Bear

Tressie Lockwood

ISBN 978-1-937394-02-8

Amira Press
Charlotte, North Carolina
www.amirapress.com

STRIPPED *Bear*

CHAPTER ONE

Ayana threw her arms up in the air and danced around in a circle. She'd finally done it. She'd purchased her first house, all on her own, four hundred miles away from the rest of her family. None of them thought she could do it. They looked at her like she wasn't capable, like she'd never be anything in life, but she'd proven them all wrong. And her house was cute too. A sweet little square brick home with the second floor holding a big sunny room where she could work on her art, along with a bathroom and an office. If her family ever came down to North Carolina to see what she was up to, she would give them a look as if to say "now, what, bitches."

She giggled at the thought and checked her mailbox just for the fun of it. As she stood next to the boring metal box, she wondered if she could find someone to build one of those brick ones to match her house. That would be perfect.

"Hello," someone called just down the street.

She glanced around and once again was struck by the quiet block with residential houses all along it. The entire area was so unlike New York, she couldn't be happier. The woman who'd called to her waved, and Ayana waited for her and her friend to draw closer. The two were about her age, maybe a little older. Both were Caucasian, another bonus to the area—mixed-race neighborhood.

"Good morning," she called out. "I'm Ayana, your new neighbor." She held out her hand, and each woman took it in turn, speaking their names. Ayana sucked at remembering names. In fact, she was so convinced that she wouldn't remember these ladies without hearing them a few times, she didn't catch what they said the first time.

The one with the long fiery red hair glanced past her to the house behind her. "Oh you bought this place?" They shared a look with each other, each appearing annoyed. Ayana almost took a step back when they then examined her from head to foot. She blinked in disbelief. Seeing Ayana ready to get her hackles up, the woman spoke again. "Oh, you'll love it around here. Everyone's friendly and down to earth."

"Yeah," the other one chipped in. Then she seemed hopeful. "Are you married?"

Ayana hesitated and crossed her arms over her chest. These women had some issues, and she couldn't put her finger on it just yet, but she was going to. She didn't think it was about race either, which was a relief. And the scan of her figure from head to toe didn't have lust in it like they were into women. There was something else. "No, I'm not. I'm single."

That hit it. If they had feathers, they would most definitely be ruffled right about now. The dark-haired one spoke again. "She's single. Well, I guess it's our duty to warn you about Brooke just in case you have a boyfriend."

The last part of her statement sounded more like a question, but this time, Ayana wasn't rising to it. They could find out on their own that she was between relationships right now. The two of them didn't seem pleased that she wasn't married.

"What about Brooke?" she asked. "Who is that?" Funny, she hadn't seen this third woman yet, but she was pretty sure she'd remember her name. Just because of the weird vibe she was getting off these ladies.

Dark Hair pointed to the house across the street, on the end. "She lives over there. If you have a man, she'll try to sleep with him. She claims to have slept with every available man in the neighborhood, and when she's drunk, she even hits on a few of the older teenagers." They both shivered in disgust. "Just steer clear, is my advice."

"Yeah," Fiery Red agreed. "Well, come on, Janet. We better continue our walk before it gets too hot. See you later, Ayana. Welcome to Lawnwood Drive."

They didn't wait for her to respond but swung around in the direction they'd been walking. Ayana's lips tightened at the comment she was sure they meant for her to hear. "We have nothing to worry about. She's too plain to be competition."

Ayana returned to her house and climbed over boxes to get to the living room. She dug around for her purse and pulled out her cell phone. The decision to get the extended plan, which included Internet service on it, was a good one. The cable company wouldn't get out to set her up with the bundle she'd purchased for another couple of days, and she needed to locate a grocery store. There wasn't a scrap of food in the house, and she was getting hungry.

Twenty minutes later, she strolled around the grocery store pushing a cart. Fresh fruit was better than her old standby granola bars. She should buy chicken instead of hamburger, but damn now that she had a backyard, how could she resist grilling good old-fashioned beef.

"I'd go with the beef," a male voice suggested when she pondered long in the meat section. A chill went down her spin at his deep timbre. She peeked up between a lock of hair that had flopped across her face and focused on the man now standing in front of her. *Talk about Prime Grade A!*

He was stocky with thick muscles in all the right places—chest and arms. His eyes were russet brown with gold flecks. A slight smile teased lips a woman could kiss all night and beg for more. In a word, he was gorgeous with a capital G. Ayana had to hold onto the cart with both hands to keep from running her fingers through his hair. The silky locks were a mess like he'd stuffed his head into a T-shirt and run out to the store just like she did. Maybe he didn't have a woman at home to cook for him. She frowned at the thought, because how likely was that. Not all this yummy goodness. A woman would have to be blind not to have snatched him up fast.

"I'm sorry," he said, breaking into her thoughts. "I didn't mean to annoy you."

She realized she'd frowned thinking about someone else getting him first. "Oh no, it's fine. You didn't annoy me." She offered her best smile and focused on his handsome face to be sure she didn't miss the name. *Man, I hope he lives close by.* "I just had so much on my mind what with just moving around here. I'm Ayana."

He put his hand out, and like a robot, she dropped hers into his palm. Her heart hammered in her chest and then felt like it had stopped when he gave her hand a gentle squeeze. "Pretty name."

Somehow she felt disappointed that he didn't give her a compliment along with the comment about her name. If she went by the interest in his eyes though, he was feeling more than her moniker. "Thanks," she breathed. He didn't let go, and she darn sure wasn't going to make him.

"Welcome to the neighborhood. I'm Reece. Tell me it's my lucky day and that your new house is near here?" His eyebrows rose in question.

Reece. Yum! Should she tell him the street? Why not? She wanted to see more of him, and it was obvious he had no problem with her race. "Lawnwood Drive." He drew in a sharp breath and named the number of her house exactly. She gasped. "How did you know?"

"For one thing, I live on that street. For another, I knew the house next door to me had been sold." He moved in closer to her. Ayana's breath caught in her throat. She didn't think her heart would slow down any time soon. Everything inside of her screamed touch him, but she wasn't getting arrested her first day here for attacking Mr. McHottie. Of course every woman within eyesight of him would understand the temptation.

Then she realized what he'd said. He lived next door to her? No way. Too, too lucky. "Next door?" she squeaked.

He nodded. "Yes, 6504."

So that's what it was, she mused. That's why the two women from earlier had gotten their feathers up. She bet every woman in the block was lusting over Reece, and to have new blood move into the area, they were worried. Of course, they'd dismissed her out of hand, like a man this hot wouldn't look twice at her. Wouldn't they cuss up a storm if they saw her right now?

She brightened her smile even more. Not that she expected him to fall for her, because seriously, men didn't land in her lap like that. She knew she was just ordinary looking. At least she had a decent figure, if a little smallish in the boob and butt area. So what. She liked to think she made up for it in personality—most of the time. "Well, it'll be nice getting to know you."

"You can count on it. In fact," he said, eying the meat selection next to them, "since you're so keen on beef, why don't you invite me over to cook out. We can consider it a house-warming. I'll bring you a gift."

Ayana laughed. He did not just invite himself over to her house so she could cook for him. Like she was going to say no. "Sure, I'd like that."

He grinned, revealing even white teeth. She resisted a bit of light-headedness. The man had all kinds of charm, and he knew it. "Is tomorrow evening too soon?"

An image of her wrecked living room slid into her head with wall-to-wall boxes. "Not at all. Sounds great."

"Good." He lifted her hand to his mouth and kissed it. Flaming hot desire scorched a path between her legs. Another look from him seemed to say he knew how she felt. "Until then."

He bent to pick up the basket he'd been carrying and turned and walked away. Ayana watched his ass in the jeans he wore and sagged against the side of the meat freezer. Moving to North Carolina was the best decision she'd ever made in her life!

CHAPTER TWO

Ayana had been speculating about which house on either side of her was the one Reece lived in. There was a forest green pickup in the one driveway and a black SUV in the other. Either of those could be a man's choice for driving, and she hadn't seen Reece come home after she got back to her place. After peeking out the window constantly in between unpacking, at least she caught sight of the mailman when he passed. She hadn't been expecting to get anything, but he'd stuff something in there.

She slipped her feet into some flip-flops and headed outside. The trek down the drive to the street filled her with excitement. If this was her apartment back home, by now some idiot would have whistled at her bare legs in the short shorts she'd slipped on to clean. And blaring music would have been coming from somebody's place with no regard to who was disturbed. Instead, she was met with peaceful quiet.

She pulled open the slot to the mailbox and retrieved a bunch of junk mail. Ah well, even that couldn't dampen her mood. A door opened somewhere behind her. Ayana's pulse kicked into high gear. She turned slowly, trying to look casual. The man standing in the doorway watching her with a curious expression on his handsome face was not Reece.

Holy cow, two in the same neighborhood. What do they put in the drinking water down here?

The man left his doorway to walk toward her as if he was on a mission. His stance the way he bore down on her held determination or like he was being pulled. Ayana didn't know whether to stand her ground or make for the house. She settled on planting her feet. When he drew up, she had to throw her head way back to look him full in the face. Goodness, he rivaled Reece in height and size, but she couldn't say either man was more handsome. This one was darker, with black hair and eyes to Reece's shades of brown. He seemed dangerous, slightly angry, although she couldn't have put her finger on why.

He raised a huge pawlike hand to her hair and grasped a few strands. *Dude, invasion of personal space much?*

"You're very small," he said.

She considered whether it was an insult and decided he was in awe. Wow, two big, sexy men mesmerized by her appearance. *Who'd have thunk it?* "Yeah, I take after my mother," she told him, a hand on her hip. "But hey, I've got her by a couple inches at least. She's five four."

He nodded as if he was gathering info on her. His next words confirmed it. "And your name?"

He was somewhat brash and simplistic in his speech, not as charming as Reece. More untamed and slightly scary. She was hooked on him already. "Ayana. And you?"

"Blaine."

Man oh man, she could enjoy his hard body, and even if he didn't have much to say, who cared. She could look at him and feel his touch. She knew she was being shallow, but hell, who was deep when they first met someone? Not with looking at Reece and Blaine they weren't. Ayana remembered the women she'd met and glanced around the street. No one was about, and she guessed now that it was later in the day, everyone had already gone to work. She'd driven during the night and arrived at her new place early.

Sudden inspiration struck her. She didn't know why she'd even consider it, and maybe it was wrong, but leaving Blaine out of the invite to her "house-warming" seemed wrong. "Blaine, I'm having a sort of house-warming tomorrow night." She laughed a little, self-conscious.

"Guess it's not really much of a house-warming since no one's coming but Reece. I thought you might like to join us. You know him?"

His dark gaze flicked to the house on the other side of hers, confirming which belonged to Reece. When he looked back at her, she caught again the determination in him. "I'd love to. Should I bring something?"

"Just yourself," she teased. And then all her bravado left at having a dinner with only two men invited. She turned back toward the house. "I'll see you then. Five-ish, I guess."

He caught her hand as she moved away and stopped her. Ayana glanced over her shoulder. His dark gaze flicked over her form, and she'd never felt more aware of her femininity and her lack of curves. Still he seemed turned-on by what he saw. She didn't dare look too low to find the evidence.

"Wear something like that," he said.

Ayana's eyebrow rose. The man had just commanded her. Not like suggestion, but an actual do it. She had to admit the dominance turned her on, but he didn't know her like that. "Wear what?" she said anyway.

He nodded toward her ass. "Those shorts."

For the second time, she waited for the compliment that didn't come. This time she did look down at the front of his black jeans. Oh yeah, he liked what he saw all right. Big, big package. Ayana bit down on her cheek, pulled her hand free, and raced into the house. She shut the door and pressed against it while her chest rose and fell at a rapid pace. Just what had she gotten herself into? They might expect something from her with her only inviting them. What about her? Did *she* expect something?

She hadn't talked much with Blaine. But it was all animal magnetism with him, barely controlled sexual need. She'd never felt so desired—in seconds no less. Maybe he had a thing for black girls. That would be a good. But she didn't want to give up Reece's charm and sweetness either. She chewed her thumbnail and looked at it. The polish was a mess. She needed to find a nail place that was good. Did she have time between now and tomorrow to do that and get the house in order? Probably not.

Sighing, she got back to work. Well with her looking like she did, plain as can be, both men practically sopped her up with gravy and a biscuit. If she improved even a little bit, they'd be into her. With that settled, Ayana threw herself harder into her tasks while fantasizing about tomorrow night. If nothing else, it would be an experience to remember.

CHAPTER THREE

Ayana plopped a huge grilled steak on Blaine's plate and one on Reece's. Then she filled their bowls with salad and made sure they had their choice of dressings and steak sauce. "Beer, soda, or sweet tea?" she called at the back door leading into the house.

"Beer," they answered in unison.

She nodded and went to grab them a cold one each. Good thing she'd picked up a couple six packs. She didn't drink beer but had opted on sweet tea. The brand she'd found in Walmart was insanely good, and she was already becoming addicted to it. After making her plate with smaller portions, she sat down across from them at the patio table she'd sprung for.

"This is delicious," Reece said while tucking a bite into his mouth. A bit of sauce stained his bottom lip, and she wanted to lick it off. He winked as if he wouldn't mind, and she looked away.

"Thanks," she murmured. "I didn't do it much back home, but I love grilled food.

"Where are you from?" he asked.

"New York. It's so different down here," she gushed. "I'm loving it already.

"Good," Blaine chimed in. "That way we don't have to hunt you down and bring you back in case you decide to leave." His smile didn't take away from the serious feel to his words.

Reece thumped his arm. "Don't mind him. You've already won this bear's heart just feeding him." Blaine gave him a sharp look, but Reece just laughed. "I'm from right here in North Carolina, all of my family as well. We have no need to go anywhere else at the moment."

"And I'm from South Carolina. I have no family," Blaine said. Her heart constricted for him. That must be hard. Even with her family getting on her last nerve, they were there for her. She'd never asked for help, but she liked to think they would step in if she needed it.

Ayana reached across the table and squeezed his forearm. A zing of pleasure went through her, and she tried pretending it was nothing. Something told her the intensity in Blaine's eyes was put there by her touch. The way they were connecting so fast, and so hot for each other, was just weird. The two of them didn't even vie for her attention. They acted like it was a done deal that they'd share. The thought of it sent a thrill through her, but that was crazy. People did that kind of thing in porn movies, not real life.

"Don't worry," she told Blaine to cover her embarrassment and the direction her mind was taking, "you've got a new friend in me, and I'm sure Reece is here for you, right?" She looked at Reece. The amusement in his eyes watching Blaine turn red made him sexier. Between the two of them, she'd never get her body to calm down.

To combat her desire, she hopped to her feet and hurried over to the chair by the back door where she'd set her CD player. After skimming through a few songs, she found the one she wanted and called over her shoulder, "Hey, y'all like hip-hop?"

They tossed her blank stares, and she laughed. Blaine volunteered, "I like Lil' Wayne."

Ayana choked, eyes wide. "You lying!" She laughed again and looked at Reece. Maybe she was being stereotypical, but she'd expected him to say he liked country or at the least some white boy rock stuff, but Lil' Wayne. "You too, Reece?"

He cringed. "No."

She flipped on the song, and beats filled the late afternoon air, not too loud to disturb the neighbors but enough for them to dance too. She ran over to grab their hands. "Come on. Dance with me."

When she'd gotten them to their feet, she raised her arms and snapped her fingers while dancing backward. They followed, their eyes glued to her gyrating hips. Obedient little puppies, they tried dancing with her, but Ayana had to fight not to fall on the ground cracking up. Neither one had an idea where the beat was, but they tried the best they could, moving stiffly like it hurt.

"Oh wow, you need so much help," she teased looking at Reece push his pelvis forward like he was the King himself. She rested a hand lightly on her head while she grooved over to him. He took hold of her hips just as she wanted him to. "Yeah, like that. Move with me."

Reece followed well. He closed the gap between them, and her breasts brushed his chest. Sweet lust took a hold on her, but before she could make him back off, Blaine closed in from behind. He didn't follow her lead as well, but the man didn't have to. His hard thigh brushed her ass, and she was no more good. Ayana broke free of the two of them and hurriedly turned the music down lower.

"Okay, that was more than I was ready for." She made a beeline for the table and sat down. "You should finish your food before it gets cold.

She didn't have to look up to know they both watched her, and Reece was the first to follow her suggestion. He sat and cleared his plate in seconds then pushed it away. "Have you ever considered a threesome?" he blurted.

Ayana had taken a sip of her tea when he spoke. She coughed. The liquid sprayed the table, and Blaine was around it in the blink to pat her back. Despite his bulky size, his touch was gentle. He didn't pound too hard. Her throat was soon clear, and she mopped her mouth and eyes with a napkin. "Thanks," she croaked.

"I'm sorry. I didn't mean to startle you," Reece said.

She glared at him. "Really? Because that came out of nowhere."

"Did it?" His golden gaze captured her attention, not letting it go. "You've seen from the first moment we all met, there's a connection. You want us as much as we want you. And we're all adults here."

"Yeah, that's what people always claim when they want to chuck their morals to the curb," she groused. "I have to live in this neighborhood, and I'm not trying for the slut on the block title."

"Don't worry. That title has already been taken."

Ayana blinked at Blaine, the irritation in his expression plain. She remembered the warning she'd gotten from the women yesterday, that she should watch out for Brooke. So even these two knew about her. She looked from one to the other as they watched her. Of course Brooke knew about these two fine specimens of manhood. She'd probably…

"Did you two have a threesome with Brooke?" She could have bitten her lip off for saying anything. Jealousy raged in her heart at the mere thought. What they'd done before she came was their business. She certainly wasn't going to share details of her sexual history, except for the fact that she was clean. Her lashes lowered, and she shredded her napkin in her hands. "You do not have to answer that. I shouldn't have asked."

"She doesn't interest us," Blaine admitted.

He stood up and brought his chair around to set it beside hers, and he took her hand in his. Chills raced over her skin when he began running his fingertips along her forearm. She squeezed her legs together. Blaine leaned in close to her ear, and his breath warmed her. "Thank you for wearing the shorts."

She'd been bold wearing the white ones with the cuff on the ends. If she bent over, half her ass would be exposed. How could they *not* think she was ready to jump in bed with them? But she'd always dressed sexy for her own enjoyment, and she played up what little she had in the way of a shape. She liked the sense of power it gave her when she went out, seeing the look of appreciation in others' eyes, even more so with Reece and Blaine.

"I'm not going to deny I like the two of you, and it blows me away that you're not fighting over me seeing who can get me. It's like you have this unspoken agreement." She eyed them. "Or did you talk about it already, agreeing to both have me? Do you share women all the time?"

Reece stood up. She couldn't read what he was thinking anymore. Even the open attraction he'd shown all day was hidden. "Let the past be past, my beautiful Ayana. We're not going to pressure you. We'll get to know each other, have a little fun. If it leads to a new experience between the three of us, great. If not, well…"

He shrugged. Somehow she didn't think that possibility really entered his mind. As far as Reece was concerned, the way she'd been acting like a woman in heat, it was just a matter of time. Blaine's expression seemed to say the same. But he was less eloquent. He lifted her chin with one beefy hand and kissed her on the lips. Nothing too passionate, no tongue, just a peck. Still it left her shaken.

At the gate leading to the front of the house, Reece paused and also gave her a chaste kiss and whispered. "I'll call you." And they were both gone.

Ayana went into the house forgetting all the leftover food, the dishes, and everything. She flopped face first on the couch and lay there unmoving. When she couldn't breathe, she turned her head to stare at her blank TV screen. They hadn't come in the house, so she'd cleaned up like a mad woman for nothing. But that wasn't what numbed her brain. What had her forgetting how to function was having two sexy men wanting her, ready to fulfill the fantasy that probably every woman had and few got to experience. She must be insane for even considering it, but she would. Oh, she *so* would!

CHAPTER FOUR

Ayana packed the last of the food she'd prepared in a basket and wiped her hands. She took everything to sit on the table beside the front door and then checked her appearance in the mirror above it. Today she wore a sundress. While it was short enough to reveal half her thighs, she didn't think it screamed "do me now" as much as the shorts had a few days ago. Something told her that wouldn't stop Reece and Blaine from lusting over her, but that wasn't a bad thing.

With a grin of happiness spreading over her face, she grabbed her sweater and opened the front door. Brooke was just crossing the street headed in her direction. Ayana sighed. The only reason she knew the woman was Brooke was because Reece had pointed her out. All thoughts of him and Blaine having a threesome with her had left the building. *Yeah, probably not*, she thought.

Brooke wasn't unattractive really. Just not the stuff of fantasies. The way everyone had talked about her, Ayana had thought she was drop-dead gorgeous and had single and married men begging for one night in her bed. The woman was instead a lush. She drank until she was drunk, and when that happened, she was silly and sex hungry rolled into one. Her figure was round, and she wore round dresses. Ayana had always felt a woman should accentuate her figure no matter her size, not downplay it. So odd that Brooke would be running behind men and offering herself to them while at the same time dressing in what amounted to quality tents.

With all that in mind, Ayana did not want to talk to her. She'd known plenty of women in New York who were man hungry and who would do anything to get one. She'd also known plenty of drunks. Not her idea of fun.

Halfway across the street, Brooke waved her arm in greeting as if they were old friends. "Hey, girl." Why did those two little words remind Ayana of Drew Barrymore in *Never Been Kissed* when she was trying to look like a cool high school student. Brooke looked nothing like Drew. Her hair was long and straight, dark brown and parted down the center. Her skin was pale like she didn't spend much time in the sun or maybe she couldn't tan at all.

Ayana was about to greet her despite her feeling when out of nowhere Blaine stood next to her. He moved in front of her so she could only see his broad back and nothing more. For a minute, she thought she heard a low growl like that of an animal, but she dismissed it. This was the suburbs, not the country for goodness sake, and most people kept their animals on a leash. She'd never seen a stray dog in this neighborhood.

When she heard no more from Brooke, she stepped around Blaine to just catch Brooke disappearing into her house and slamming the door. Ayana wrinkled her nose. "Okay, that was weird. You'd think she'd have run over here faster seeing you. But whatever." She put a possessive hand on his arm without thinking about it. "Ready for our picnic?"

He smiled down at her, apparently not a care in the world. "Definitely. Did you cook?"

She laughed. "I'm getting the feeling you like me for my food, man. So not good."

"Oh no," He swooped her into a strong embrace that took her off her feet. Her heart raced when he leaned down and kissed her. "You have a lot more I want than just food."

Ayana almost toppled with overstimulation when he set her down again. And Reece strolled up just in time to steady her. She tipped her head back to thank him as he stood behind her with his hands on her shoulders. Her breath snagged in her chest just looking from him to Blaine and back again.

"Thanks," she murmured.

Reece ran a thumb across her cheek and then patted her ass, turning her in the direction of his SUV. "Any time. Let's get going, huh?"

Ayana grumbled, but she did as he asked. "Don't do that out here. Anyone could see."

He raised his eyebrows at her as he climbed into the driver seat and her on the passenger side. "Are you ashamed of us?"

"Please. What woman would be? No, I just know Brooke's watching us through her window. Everybody in the neighborhood will be talking about me going out with the two of you and come to the conclusion that I'm doing you both."

"I'm not opposed to making that true," Reece teased as he pulled out of the drive.

"Me either," Blaine quipped from the back seat.

She rolled her eyes at them while she clicked her seatbelt into place. "Well, I haven't decided to take you up on that offer. What if I'm more interested in one of you, rather than the other?" She knew she'd asked them the same question over and over for the last few days, but the truth was she was scared to take that step. Just looking at them told her sex with them would be explosive, but what kind of woman did it with two men at once? She'd never thought she'd be that type. But Reece and Blaine were into her like no men ever had been. They'd obviously been friends for a while. She couldn't mess that up. This was a huge risk for all of them.

A short while later, Reece pulled up to the park by the lake. Ayana breathed in the fresh, warm air, enjoying the sound of the birds chirping and the shade from the trees. She stepped out of the SUV and grabbed the blanket she'd packed. When she would have pulled the basket out too, Blaine's big arm came around her waist and he hoisted her out of the way to get it himself.

She shook her head chuckling and found a spot to lay out the blanket. In the distance, several other people had their same idea of enjoying the park, but she was glad no one was close by. Their spot felt secluded and private.

Once they were settled on the blanket, she opened the basket and began sorting through the food and drinks. "Do y'all want to eat now or later? I think it's warm enough to swim. We might want to get in the water for a while first."

Reece eyed her blouse front. "Do you have a suit on under that?"

She smirked. "Well I'm not skinny-dipping if that's what you hoped for."

He tsked. "Too bad."

"What about you?" she asked, pointedly staring at his crotch. "You got swim shorts on?"

He shrugged and lay on his back with his hands tucked behind his head. "These double as swimming trunks. I'm easy. But if you want to see me naked, you have only to say the word."

"One-track mind." She twisted the cap off of a beer and handed it to him. Somehow she already felt domesticated. A second beer she passed to Blaine. He rested his back against a tree, his legs extended straight out. Seeing them crossed at the ankle was incongruent with his size. Blaine looked like the clichéd bull in a china shop, but she'd never seen him clumsy.

"Ayana, tell me about your family," Reece encouraged her.

She looked to see if he was really interested, and from his attention to her, she concluded that he was. "Nothing interesting to tell really. I have two sisters and one brother. I'm the youngest."

She must have had a funny expression on her face with the last part because he reached out and took her hand, twining his fingers between hers. "You don't get the respect you deserve because you're the youngest."

"Not exactly." She hesitated. Normally, she wouldn't talk about the differences she had with her family, but sharing it with him felt natural. "I don't bring men home often. I don't know why. I just don't, and one particular time I did, most of my family felt he wasn't about anything. Never mind that he had a job, a car, and seemed like he had money. Maybe they could sense something I didn't. I was so into him. Anyway, he showed his true colors real quick. He got his hands on my money and cleaned me out. Later, I found out he was messing with my friend, and she knew he was with me." She waved her hand. "That's a whole other story. With the help of my father and some people he knew we caught up with him."

She fell silent, staring down at the sandwiches she'd unpacked but hadn't put on plates yet. The same old embarrassment and humiliation washed over her. How could she not see what that bastard was all about? Her mother and sisters, even her cousin, had lectured her for hours, and they didn't trust her to make her own choices after that. That's why she'd moved to North Carolina, to get out from under them. Buying her house proved to them only so much that she could handle her own business.

Blaine tugged her onto his lap, and she stiffened looking around to see if anyone was looking. He wound his arms around her waist and made her lean into his big chest. A sense of protection and warmth stole over her. She didn't dare trust this because she might have shown that she could get her finances right again, but that didn't mean she wasn't still a lousy judge of men. For the time being she enjoyed him holding her.

He nuzzled her face and found her lips for a kiss. Ayana gave into it. When Blaine raised his head, she expected lust-filled eyes but found anger instead and gasped. "Where is he? What's his name?" he demanded.

She realized why he was ticked and stroked his strong jawline. "Thanks, you're so sweet. But he's serving time. After I went to trial over that asshole, so many women came out of the woodwork claiming he'd done that mess to them. He won't be doing it any time soon."

Blaine didn't seem appeased. He gritted his teeth. Reece chuckled and sat up. He grabbed a sandwich, ripped the plastic off of it, and stuffed it into his mouth. When he finished chewing, he said, "Don't tell him anything, Ayana. The idiot would hunt the man just to avenge you in his own way."

Her bear, which was what she was beginning to think of Blaine as, glared at Reece, but the other man only laughed again. They were as different as night and day, but she liked them both for that. Imagining if she had to choose between the two, she tried to figure out which one she'd go with. Reece was lighthearted and fun. He laughed and smiled easily, and conversation was usually with him and Blaine adding gruff responses in between. On the other hand, Blaine was so protective. She had no doubt he'd beat up her ex without blinking an eye if he ever came across him. Blaine's bulky size and his barely contained desire had her on fire. To be enveloped in his arms made her dizzy with happiness and contentment.

"What do you do?" she asked him over her shoulder.

"For a living?" he asked. She nodded. "Landscaper."

She waited for him to elaborate, but he didn't. She laughed. This was why she wouldn't only have Blaine as a lover. She looked over at Reece. He explained. "He's being modest. He owns his own company. The bear might not look it, but Blaine's got a good head for business and is something of an inventor. He holds two patents on some type of motor for landscaping equipment. If you could wrestle more than a sentence out of him, he could tell you all about it."

Her eyes widened. "Wow, cool." Blaine rewarded her with a hungry kiss. She had to push him back to keep herself in control. "And you, Reece?"

He'd gone back to lying down with his hands behind his head. "I'm just a lowly office worker." Blaine grunted, and Reece sighed. "Fine, I am VP of a small firm."

She blinked. "And you live on Lawnwood Drive?"

"I don't take myself or life too seriously," he responded.

She smiled. "I like that philosophy." She wiggled out of Blaine's arms and stood up. Both men watched her as she stripped off her dress. Ayana bit her bottom lip as she tugged her bikini bottom pretending not to notice how they feasted on her with their eyes. A plain woman never felt so beautiful. "I'm going for a swim. You can't come, Reece, because you just ate."

He leaped to his feet. "As if I'm not going to follow you wherever you go!" He practically tore out of his shirt and threw it on the grass. His shoes weren't far behind, and Blaine shed his clothing as well.

Ayana ran down toward the water with both of them hot on her heels.

CHAPTER FIVE

Ayana woke up on Saturday having come to a decision. She was going to go for it with Blaine and Reece. She still didn't know a whole lot about them as far as personal stuff. A search of Blaine's name on the Internet had revealed a website for his landscaping business. The man was more successful than he'd let on just as Reece said. But she wasn't planning on losing her heart. This was about sexual enjoyment, and she was so going to do just that.

After a quick shower, she perused her closet for the perfect outfit to wear and then wondered if she shouldn't just choose something she didn't care a lot about. Something told her the minute she let Blaine know she was open to having sex with him, the man would rip her clothes off.

A tingle passed over her spine just thinking that. She'd never had a lover so aggressive as to go that far. But what woman hadn't fantasized about a hot man grabbing hold of her panties and tearing them into scraps of cloth. *So sexy.*

She imagined both Reece and Blaine doing it and then chastised herself. Rather than falling into a fantasy, she could have the real thing. So long as they were both still on board with sharing. After showering and brushing her teeth, she selected a minidress of butter yellow, which set off her mocha skin nicely. She slipped her feet into sandals and jogged downstairs to the first floor of her house.

Ayana could call but why delay things when she could be at one of her men's front door in seconds. Peeking outside, she made sure the coast was clear as far as neighbors and then felt childish. She raised her chin and flung the door open to step out. *Damn, now which one?*

Did she prefer one over the other? Not really. They both had their pluses. Both tugged at her desire to feel his hands on her body. At a roadblock, she stood there thinking. Not until Reece's door opened was the decision taken out of her hands.

He strolled across the half lawn expanse that separated their houses. "What are you doing out here just standing around?" he asked, amusement in his eyes.

Ayana put a hand on her hip and offered him a sassy smile. "I was trying to think which of you gets to know first that I'm ready."

Reece stood stock still in front of her, staring. "By ready, you mean…"

She nodded.

Disbelief and excitement mingled in his eyes. "Are you sure?"

"Positive." She tugged at the strings that tied the top of her dress and played with them. "Do you like my dress?"

His gaze was like a full-body lick from her feet to her head as he scanned her entire form. "Very much. Now, you go inside your house. I'll call Blaine."

She wanted to ask why she had to go back in the house, but he turned her at the shoulders and gave her a little push forward. When she stepped over her entryway, she glanced back to find him returning to his own house. Ayana frowned. She supposed he wanted to clean up some and then he'd be back over. He could knock on the door. She shut it and began pacing. This was more of a production than she expected. This situation had taken too much thought, and now it felt like planning. Shouldn't they have spontaneously fallen into bed all together?

While she considered it, the next knock she heard came from the back door rather than the front. Now she got what Reece had been doing. He knew she was still worried about what people thought in the block, so he'd used the back door and probably got Blaine to do it as well.

Now that they were here, her stomach knotted painfully. She swallowed wishing she had a glass of water, but her legs were too rubbery and her hands shook too much for her to answer the door and handle a glass at the sink.

She opened the door to both men, and they stepped inside her kitchen. All of a sudden the space she'd thought was just enough for her seemed more like a closet. Blaine and Reece both big men took up all the room in the area and towered above her. Her eyes widened, and she stumbled backward. Reece threw out a hand to steady her.

"Hey, easy, we can take this as slow as you need. Okay?" he said.

She nodded, not trusting herself to say a word or they'd know how nervous she was. Of course with the buggy eyes, they probably had a clue. She led the two of them upstairs to her bedroom, and while she stood next to her bed, Blaine shut the door. Reece moved closer to her and ran a gentle hand along her jawline. Ayana's breath caught in her throat. But soon her desire moved past her fear, and she remembered just how much she wanted these men.

Reece seemed to sense her rise in awareness of him. He opened his arms, and she stepped into them. Her palms flattened against his chest, and she tilted her head to the side as he searched out the sensitive skin at her neck.

Ayana shuddered and closed her eyes. "How can you know just the spot…?"

The tip of his tongue delved into the hollow at the base of her neck, just onto her shoulder. Tremors of delight passed through her. But before she could totally lose herself in what Reece was doing, Blaine came up. He tapped Reece, and Reece stepped aside as if they were doing a tag team thing. She melted into Blaine's big arms. His loving was miles different from Reece's. He hoisted her into his arms with her legs wrapped around his waist. His invasion of her mouth with his tongue was not a question of was she ready but a demand to give it up now.

Ayana's body flamed to life. She didn't protest when Blaine laid her on the bed and followed with a knee between her legs. Her heart pounded in her chest. She licked her lips as she watched him raise her dress. Just like she'd imagined, Blaine curled his fingers around the delicate material of her panties and snatched them off. They tore apart under his huge hands, and she had to bite down on a moan.

"You big oaf," Reece growled. "I told her we would take it slow."

Blaine glared at him. "How can I when I can smell her come wetting her pussy?"

This time, Ayana did moan. Blaine's rough words set her off. She wriggled on the bed as he laid a hand on her thigh. He was going to go down on her. She knew it, and he looked hungrier for it than any of her previous lovers. All of them had done it because they wanted to be sucked in return. Blaine's expression said he didn't care if she did suck him. He wanted to lick her pussy as much as he liked. Who was she to stop him?

"I'm okay, Reece," she said and looked up at him. He studied her face and then bent down to kiss her. When he raised his head, he took hold of her leg and lifted it. The movement gave Blaine greater access to her pussy. Ayana cried out at the first touch of his tongue. He laved her from the bottom of her moist folds to the top. He scooped her opening taking her come into his mouth. She writhed and murmured his name. "Oh, Blaine, what are you doing?"

Reece whistled as he watched his friend eat her. "Mm, yeah eat her, Blaine. Make our Ayana come."

His encouragement made her all the more hot. The actions of Blaine's tongue were torment, especially when he closed his lips over her sensitive bud and began sucking. She all but screamed and tried to pull away. Reece held her in place, staring into her eyes. He held her captive with those gold depths.

"Reece," she whispered.

"No, you don't, baby. It's good, isn't it? You like it?" He pushed her dress higher, exposing her small breasts. She couldn't help hoping he wouldn't find them unattractive, but his eyes widened as he stared down at her. "I had no idea how dark your areolas are. They look like chocolate. Are your nipples sweet?"

"Find out," she said with shaky boldness.

Reece didn't waste time sampling her nipples. They were already rigid peeks, but his tongue swirling around the edges and then his lips pulling them into his mouth to suckle made them ache. She arched into his touch, closing her eyes while pushing her fingers into his hair.

"Mm, I can't believe…" she stuttered, "at the same time…" She pumped her hips against Blaine's mouth and lifted her head to watch as Reece tease her breasts. Her orgasm was building fast. The stimulation was overwhelming, but Reece laid a hand on her belly to keep her in place. Blaine's grunts as he sucked on her clit were the final straw. She screamed. Her core muscles tightened. Her climax shattered all ability to do anything other than lie there and enjoy. She whimpered their names as her muscles spasmed.

Blaine reached under her and cupped her ass cheeks in both hands. He lifted her hips to catch every drop of her cream as it dripped down her channel. His hunger didn't abate until she'd shivered through a second orgasm and then a third. At last, he raised his head and sat up. Ayana gasped and blinked when she thought his face was different like it had shifted to someone or some*thing* else, but Reece moved in front of his friend before she could be sure the lust hadn't been playing tricks on her mind.

"Are you ready for me?" Reece asked.

She wanted to look around him to check Blaine, but then Reece opened his slacks. This time, Ayana could have whistled in appreciation at the size of his cock. Reece was long with a nice girth. His cock was slightly curved, and it was rock-hard. Her breath came out in pants as she stared at him. Ayana pulled her dress up over her head. She tossed it to the floor and lay back against the pillows.

Reece's eyes blazed with his desire. He shed his clothes and pulled out a condom packet from his pocket. While he rolled it onto his cock, Blaine stood up to take his clothes off as well. Ayana stared at him, but he appeared normal. She'd been imagining things. All thought of him having changed left her mind. Blaine's cock matched his stocky size. He was so thick, it scared her a little about taking him inside her. But hell, she wasn't turning him down.

"Come here," she said, holding her hand out.

Blaine's eyebrow went up at her command, but he came closer to the bed. She wrapped her fingers around his thickness and stroked. Blaine's breath hissed between his teeth. Ayana waited until Reece held her legs up and pushed the head of his cock into her pussy. Her fingers spasmed on Blaine's cock, squeezing him. He groaned in pleasure.

"Yes," she cried out. "Give it to me."

Reece pushed her legs even higher so that her ass rose off the bed as he seated himself deeper into her pussy. She groaned and wiggled. The contracting of her core made her feel like she was going to come again, but she willed it to hold. Reece drove in as deep as he could and then pulled out. The sensation was too good to be over too soon. He grunted with each entry. "Oh, baby, you're so wonderfully tight. I wish I could get every inch in you."

"Try," she begged. But he was too long, at least nine inches. He moved with precision even though he quickened his pace. He knew how far to go without bumping her cervix. While he pinched her hips in a strong grip, he thrust into her pussy. Ayana called out his name.

Her lust increased so much, she had a craving to taste Blaine in her mouth. She looked up at him and found he watched her with dark, almost black eyes. Her lips parted at the danger she saw there, but she wasn't scared so much as nervous about Blaine's strength. He put a knee on the bed and moved closer. He caught her under the chin and tugged his cock from her fingers. A thrill passed over her when Blaine fed her his cock. She had to open her mouth wide to get his thick head between her lips. Precome flavored her tongue.

"Suck it hard," he insisted. She obeyed, taking it a bit deeper and pulling on his length at the same time. Blaine groaned. Soon she was lost in squeezing his shaft in her fist while Reece pounded between her legs. He was the one that let go first, shouting her name and throwing his head back as his hips rocked against her.

Reece kept up a slow pump into her pussy while she sucked hard at Blaine's cock. He pulled him out and licked his thick head, swirling her tongue around the tip. He tangled his fingers in her hair and tugged a little, but Reece growled, "Easy with her."

She looked up at her bear of a lover and knew that it was taking everything he had to keep control. She'd been right about Blaine having a danger about him. She was still too turned on to be afraid of him.

"Do you want to try DP, Ayana?" Reece asked.

Her eyes widened. She knew just what DP meant but felt kind of embarrassed to admit it. "DP?"

He grinned. "Double penetration. The big guy will fill your sweet pussy, while I'm in the back." She was about to reach out to stroke him to be sure he was ready, but the man hadn't gone down at all. His shaft was erect. He'd discarded the condom and was preparing another. Something told her taking on the two of them was going to wear her out. But hell what woman would turn down this opportunity?

"Yes," she breathed, and she sat up. Reece replaced her in the position on her back, and Blaine hoisted her like she weighed nothing on top of his friend. A shiver of anticipation brought goose bumps to the surface of Ayana's skin. She watched as Blaine lifted her legs and held them high. He dipped two fingers into her pussy and made sure they were good and coated with her thick juices before teasing the hole at the back. Her eyes fluttered closed when he pushed in one then two fingers. She squirmed and whimpered, loving the feel of it. A tight fit, but it didn't hurt at all. She loved anal sex and enjoyed it with most of her past lovers.

"Tell me you like that, Ayana," Blaine commanded.

She moaned. "I like it. Don't stop."

He didn't. He worked her anus while Reece played with her clit. With his other hand he turned her head so he could capture her lips, and she surrendered herself to him. Reece stuck his tongue between her lips and swirled in the warm depths. She greedily kissed him back, seeking to experience more of his flavor.

"She's ready," Blaine announced, and Reece lost no time in guiding his cock head between her ass cheeks. Ayana gasped and groaned, but she took every inch. At least from this angle and because it was in her rear, she could take all of him.

Reece's fingers laced with hers on both sides of them. He began a slow grind that sent her flying. Ayana cried out as an orgasm careened through her system. She'd never had one with a man in her butt alone, but Reece had taken her there. Still, the pleasure wasn't over. Blaine had put on a condom as well, and he pushed his cock head between her slick folds.

"Slowly," Reece barked, as if he either felt it or sensed what Blaine was doing.

"I'd never hurt her," Blaine said, but he wasn't exactly gentle. His thick shaft pierced her and ground deep fast. Ayana's teeth chattered. Another orgasm took hold, aftershocks. They fit so snug, and the sensation was so much she didn't know whether to moan or faint. She could do nothing but lie there allowing these two fine men to assault her body. They moved in unison thrusting into her pussy and ass, and then they moved at odds, first one, then the other. Blaine withdrew, and then Reece. Blaine pounded into her, and Reece followed.

Ayana screamed her pleasure. She'd never been a screamer either, but this was beyond anything she'd ever felt. "Stop," she begged. "No, don't stop. Don't ever stop!"

Her mind was in a whirl. This was all too much and not enough. Neither man gave into her pleas except to keep driving into her over and over. Ayana came for the millionth time. She'd lost count. Blaine jerked above her. His hold on her legs slipped. Her legs came down some because she had no strength to keep them up. A tighter squeeze, and he cursed. She knew he'd climaxed and smiled with her eyes closed.

Blaine panted above her, but Reece continued to pump into her rear until he reached his second orgasm. Finally, the two of them pulled out, and she rolled to Reece's side to land on the bed in an exhausted heap. When she caught her breath, she whispered, "I never knew it could be that good. Wow…just wow."

Reece rolled over and pulled her to him while he spooned her. His heavy arm rested over her abdomen. "There's plenty more where that came from."

She eyed him over her shoulder and Blaine who was discarding his used condom from an erect shaft. "Why do I feel like you two can go many more hours?"

Reece chuckled. "I don't know." He rubbed against her. She felt his shaft push against her rear. The man still hadn't gotten enough. A thrill shot through her. Well neither had she.

"Different positions?" she suggested hopefully.

Blaine climbed on the bed and scooped her into his arms. "Every way, until I have sampled every inch of your beautiful body."

"Mm," Ayana cooed. "Let's get started.

CHAPTER SIX

Ayana had kicked the two men out of her house sometime around midnight. The sun had risen hours ago, but she'd been unable to move a muscle. Now that it was past noon, she struggled to her feet and winced toward the bathroom. Off and on all day yesterday, the three of them had made love. The only time they'd let her off her back or off their laps was to go get something to eat. Not that she'd been complaining. No way. If she was going to have two men at once, she was going to enjoy every second.

However, today, she was paying for her wantonness. Sore muscles and guilt. Too many women out in the world were looking for a good man, and she'd selfishly taken two. She ran the shower until the water was hot but tolerable and stepped inside. Okay, so the thought that she shouldn't be stingy passed through her mind, but she wasn't certain she was ready to give Blaine and Reece up. Not for some mystery woman, certainly not for one of the women in the block who'd had plenty of chances before she moved down there.

Alrighty-then, Ayana, you've officially gone insane with too much sex.

She grinned. When she made them leave, they still had desire in their eyes. They were like insatiable animals, and it turned her on just seeing how much looking at her got them hard. This was a dream to be enjoyed for the time being. Not for a moment did she think it could lead anywhere.

She ran her hands over her body, kneading sore muscles where she found them. If she was honest with herself, she'd admit she could love

Blaine and Reece, maybe even felt a little something now. But that would be just that hormone thing that made a woman attached to the men she slept with. Had she screwed herself royally taking them both? What if in the end it did come down to a choice? The hormone, she suspected, wasn't choosy on its own. The thing had probably equally latched her to both men.

Ayana sighed. When she stepped out of the shower to dry off, she was resolute. A little more time. She'd let things play as they would and not question it for now. While she lotioned her skin and picked out something to wear, the doorbell rang. She frowned considering whether to hurriedly get dressed or to toss on a robe to answer it. Her clothes won out just in case it was one of her men. They didn't need to start imagining she had nothing on under the robe. Her body was so not ready for more acrobatics.

By the time she'd scrambled into a bra, panties, and a dress, she was surprised the person was still at the door when she went downstairs. *Determined much? Sheesh.*

She opened the door to find Brooke standing there, darting furtive looks to the left and right. The words *crazy* and *dramatic* trembled on Ayana's lips, but she kept her opinion to herself. "Uh, Brooke, right? You okay?"

The bold woman darted past Ayana into her house and slammed the door closed. She rested a hand on her chest, half-exposed boobs rising and falling. Ayana crinkled her nose in disgust and put a hand on her hip. *I know this heifer didn't just barge into my house uninvited.*

"Is there something I can do for you because we don't know each other well enough for you to just charge in here. In fact, we don't know each other at all," she snapped.

Brooke's face took on a pitying expression. Ayana narrowed her eyes. She'd seen enough of that from her own family. She didn't need it from someone she didn't know. Brooke didn't seem to recognize how pissed off she was. She grabbed Ayana's arm, widening overly made up eyes for early afternoon. "I'm worried about you, and I thought I should come over and warn you."

Ayana shook her hand off and smirked. "Oh, you're worried about me. Somehow I don't believe that for a second. You think I don't know your reputation?" Common sense and just plain not repeating gossip she had no evidence of should have told her to keep her mouth shut, but this woman was irritating the mess out of her. The bottom line was she was jealous, like half the women around here. Ayana wasn't delusional. She knew she didn't command sexy men's attention on a daily basis. This was special, and why shouldn't she enjoy it without heifers like this trying to tear it down. "You want them for yourself. I heard there's not a single man around here you haven't propositioned or right out slept with. What, Reece and Blaine not giving in to your offer and you're making sure no one gets them? How juvenile can you get?"

Brooke turned bright red. Her eyes narrowed. "They're dangerous. They threatened my life!"

Ayana jerked her front door open. Without a second thought, she took Brooke's arm and shoved her through the opening. "Maybe you should have called the police. Don't come to my house again, or I will have *you* arrested for trespassing."

"I saw them come out from behind your house late last night," Brooke blurted. Ayana slammed the door in her face. Before she realized she was going to do it, she started crying. Not noisy sobs, but tears streaming down her face. She had no reason to believe anything that woman had to say, but experience had taught her that she wasn't a good judge of character in men. What if there was something about them? After all, men didn't normally share their women like Reece and Blaine seemed happy to do. And she'd seen the darkness in Blaine's eyes, like he was more than what he appeared. Even though he'd been gentle with her, if rough around the edges, that didn't mean he wasn't hiding a temper.

She walked to the couch and sank down onto it to draw her knees to her chest. About to give in to a bout of self-pity, she recalled the last words Brooke said before she slammed the door in her face. Brooke had seen the guys leave her house. Of course, she was jealous, and anyone with half a brain would know what they were doing that late. She grinned and wiped her face. Relief washed over her. Okay, that whole episode had been prompted by Brooke wishing she was the one in the middle of that yummy sandwich. Whatever, she wasn't getting Reece and Blaine. For now, they were all Ayana's, and she wasn't giving them up any time soon. She would guard her heart while giving them her body. Just thinking it had her sexual desire igniting. She'd never thought she could want it as much as she did now, but the guys had turned something on in her that wouldn't be satisfied except by their touch.

She lay on her belly across the couch and reached for her cell phone. With a single button touch, she dialed Reece. He answered on the first ring. "Hey, beautiful, I was just going to call you."

She grinned. "Really? Why?"

"Missing that sexy body of yours."

She rolled her eyes and then flipped onto her back so she could look up at the ceiling. "Oh yeah? What about it?"

"Your chocolate nipples for one."

"Hmm," she responded, "yeah you do like sucking them a lot, but I'm sure they don't taste like chocolate."

"Have you tried them?" His tone had gone deeper like their conversation had begun to turn him on. That didn't stop her from hearing the other person in the room saying something about did Reece really have to talk so openly about his sex life while he was there. Ayana didn't know whether to be embarrassed or laugh at Reece's boldness. The man had no shame.

"Who was that? Where are you, Reece?"

"At work," he said. "That was my coworker, John. He has no appreciation of the fact that I can't get enough of you and I've done more talking about you than actual work today."

"Don't get in trouble on my account." She warned him, but she was still excited by the fact that he couldn't get her out of his mind. Of course, it might have been better if he thought of something other than sex, or in addition to it at least. "You should try to work so you won't get fired. I'm lucky I'm off today, but then I work from home. My boss isn't breathing over my shoulder."

"Must be very nice," he quipped. "Okay, my love, if you promise to open your sweet legs to me when I get home, I will make an attempt to be productive while I'm here." The man in the background growled Reece's name, but he only laughed. "Is it a deal?"

She sighed. "Fine, it's a deal. Now behave yourself. Bye."

"Bye." He clicked off.

Ayana sucked in another deep breath and let it go. Guard her heart. Yeah, right."

A lawnmower started up outside, and she got up to walk over to the window. When she pulled the curtain back, it was to find Blaine riding a standing mower around her front lawn. She watched as he gripped the controls, arm muscles already glistening wet from the heat of the sun. His tan was deep from being out in the elements probably all year around. When he zoomed by near her, he glanced up as if sensing her watching. The look in his eyes was possessive. She shivered both with nerves and excitement. Instinct told her Blaine would protect her no matter what the foe if ever she needed it. That was a nice thought.

She left the window and went up to the second floor where her office was. While her computer powered up, she dialed her boss. Kevin picked up on the third ring. "Hey, I thought you were off today."

"I am." She bit her lip, hesitant. "You remember you told me you have that friend in law enforcement?"

He chuckled. "My ex-girlfriend, yeah. What about her? Are you in trouble with the law, Ayana?"

She sucked her teeth. "Man, please. I'm not the one. No, I'm just hoping you're still on good terms with her. I…uh…I need a favor."

Kevin was more than her boss. He was a friend. In fact, they'd gotten to know each other online a few years ago and then had coffee and became good friends in the real world. Funny enough, there'd never been any romantic feelings between them—at least not on her part. She was pretty sure she hadn't missed any signs. But when Kevin decided to use his life savings and his expertise in web development to start up a business, he offered her the job of being his assistant. The salary spoke to her, and hell her job at the time hadn't been going well. The handwriting so to speak had been on the wall. She'd jumped at Kevin's offer, especially since the position was a work at home one. The two of them had never looked back, and she'd been right to trust Kevin's brilliant mind. His business was a huge success, and for the last three years, she'd gotten raises. That had allowed her to move away from her family to live in North Carolina.

"Seriously," Kevin insisted, "you can tell me if you're in trouble, Ayana. I'll help you no matter what."

She smiled, feeling warmed by his assertion. Kevin knew all about her disastrous past relationship, but she didn't want to go into details and hear him warn her off of a threesome with two men she didn't know. "Thanks. I just want you to see if your friend can find anything out about someone. Uh, two someones."

While she spoke, she did a quick search of public records online for Mecklenburg County. The site would share info on the owners of the two houses on either side of hers. She was in luck that both Reece and Blaine owned their houses rather than rented.

"I was wondering if you can have your friend check to see if there's anything on a Reece Covington and Blaine Shore."

"Criminal history you mean?" he asked. Her stomach knotted with guilt.

"Um, I guess." She didn't want to believe that either of them had a wrap sheet, not to mention not wanting to look into their backgrounds at all. There was such a thing as trust and violating a person's privacy. She could just ask them what she wanted to know, and she knew many people would condemn her who didn't understand the horror, the hurt, and the humiliation she'd gone through, and continued to at the hands of her loving family after what her ex-boyfriend did. No one but someone who had dealt with it could truly get how vulnerable it left a person. She couldn't just be careful or ignore her fears and just go back to the innocent thing she was back then.

Kevin spoke in a low, gentle tone. "Care to tell me what this is about?"

"Not really." She tensed waiting for him to deny her help if she wasn't going to give him details.

He sighed. "Okay, I'll see what I can find out and get back to you. If you need me, I'm always here, Ayana. You know that."

She smiled. "Yeah, I know."

"Good, now get back to enjoying your day off because I plan to work your ass tomorrow. I've got a backlog."

Ayana grunted and said her good-byes before she hung up the phone. She focused on her computer and looked up various recipes for dinner. Reece and Blaine loved food. She intended to make them a feast that would have them smacking their lips long after it was devoured. If guilt drove her to do it, she didn't let it get to her too much. She was a woman alone in a state far from family and friends. She did what she had to do.

CHAPTER SEVEN

At four, Ayana had just stepped from the shower, when she heard her cell phone ringing. With a towel wrapped around her torso, she darted for it and shivered as the cool air in the room caressed her wet skin.

"Hello?" she said, slightly out of breath.

"Ayana, what have you been doing?" Kevin teased.

"Shut up, nut." She laughed. "I was just running trying to get the phone before it stopped. "What's up?"

"I got some info on your friends."

Her eyes widened. "So fast? That was just this morning."

She could hear the shrug in his voice. "What can I say? My ex was good at a lot of things. Hm, maybe I should revisit that…"

"The info?" she interrupted, not wanting to go there with his love life.

"Oh yeah. No major issues. Blaine Shore had a run in with the law in South Carolina when he was fifteen. Joy riding."

She wrinkled her nose. "Shouldn't that have been sealed or something?"

"Maybe. I don't claim to know much about the law. Anyway, nothing after that. His record is clean. He owns a landscaping business, and all his permits and such are in order. The other one, Reece."

Butterflies formed in her stomach. "Yeah?"

"Nothing. He's even cleaner than the other guy. No record of wrongdoing. My friend said she couldn't even find out where he was from, whether it was here in NC or elsewhere. Who is he?"

"Nobody."

"Ayana."

"Just drop it, Kevin, okay?" She sighed. "Listen, I have to go. I've got something in the oven, and I don't want it to burn. Thanks a lot for looking into them for me. You're a true friend."

"I am. Ayana, I—"

"I have to go, Kevin. Thanks again." She disconnected the call not knowing if Reece with no background was a good or bad thing. He'd said he was from right there in North Carolina, but to find zilch was weird, wasn't it? Didn't the police always have at least some tidbit on a person even if they'd been a model citizen, like family home or something? Maybe Kevin's friend hadn't looked beyond criminal background. And the fact that Blaine had a business license had stuck out, while Reece's VP job was less something to track as far as the law.

Well, she might have been wrong to investigate them without asking in the first place, so since nothing serious had been found, she decided to drop it. Tonight would be fun, and for now, that's all that mattered.

She lotioned her skin and searched through her closet for something cute. She'd gone through all the short shorts she owned for Blaine's pleasure. The man couldn't get enough of looking at her ass in material that barely covered it. A sense of warmth stole over her thinking of that. She probably shouldn't like it so much, but how could anyone not? Blaine was gorgeous, and he wanted her. Ayana didn't live a life of men running behind her.

She remembered that she'd bought a white tube dress that hugged her figure to the point that she looked like she was curvier. The dress reached the middle of her thighs, and her shoulders were bare. She decided to accent it with a wide beige belt that zipped together at the back. The belt was simple but stylish enough to set off the plain dress. Strappy, medium-heeled sandals completed her outfit, and she was ready to see her men.

Right on time, one of them rang the bell at five. Ayana glanced at herself one last time in the mirror and tucked a few strands of black hair behind her ear. She'd pressed it straight and curled the ends, nothing fancy. Her makeup was light since she didn't enjoy wearing it during the warmer months. She left her bedroom and hurried downstairs to get the door. When she opened it, her breath caught. Blaine and Reece stood in the doorway looking good enough to eat.

"I thought we were doing the back door," she breathed.

Reece's eyebrows went up. "Are you ashamed of us?"

"You asked me that before." She stepped back to let them by. "I'm not. Aren't you two hot in those jeans?"

Blaine's eyes glittered as he captured her to pull into his arms as Reece shut the door. "I could strip," he said, and she knew he would.

A chill of excitement raced over her flesh. "I'm sure you could and would, but I didn't cook for nothing. Come on. You two can help me set the table. Mind if we eat inside today? The mosquitoes put me on the menu last time."

She knew she was babbling, but being in Blaine's arms had set her body on fire. And Reece had moved up behind her, reminding her of what they'd done last time. Goodness knew she wanted more of *that.* But as much as she talked and tried wiggling away, Blaine wasn't ready to let go.

"A kiss?" he asked.

She melted against his chest, surrendering. His mouth came down on hers, and he parted her lips to invade with his tongue. Arrows of need shot straight between her legs, and she knew her panties were beginning to get soaked. From behind, Reece ran his hands along her sides, raised them up and cupped her breasts. Her heart pounded. She arched, pushing her ass back, and he took the offering by pressing into her, his cock nestling against her rear.

When Blaine raised his head, she was out of breath, but Reece immediately took hold of her chin and captured her mouth with his own. Blaine didn't back away. He continued to hold her to him while he watched Reece kiss her. Ayana couldn't help the moan that escaped her lips. Reece left her mouth and kissed her cheeks, her nose, and her eyes. While he nuzzled her temple with his lips, Blaine swooped back in to tease her neck with the tip of his tongue. Ayana shuddered. Realizing this was getting out of hand, she slipped from between them and took a few steps toward the kitchen.

"The food," she rasped, hurrying away. Both men followed her silent like predators, and she couldn't shake the longing to run back into their arms.

"I like the dress." Blaine's words were direct and simple, but she heard the excitement in his tone. How odd that it would be him who was most attentive to the changes she made in her appearance more so than Reece.

She smiled wiggling her hips as she paused in front of the stove. "Thanks. Now, if you boys will set the table, we can get this party started. I'm starving."

Ayana couldn't help the feeling of being a real couple—triple?—as they worked together to get the food on the table and their place setting done. Reece and Blaine sat at each end of the small table, and she sat at the side. Neither man was shy about dishing out heaping amounts of her homemade mashed potatoes, brisket, and green beans, along with homemade biscuits smothered in butter. The whole meal was a bit much for the time of year, but it was what they requested. She had a feeling they were used to microwaving their meals or eating out. Since she loved cooking anyway, she didn't mind going all out, and they always appreciated it, which was a huge bonus.

"So," Ayana began between bites of food, "how did you two meet each other? Was it when you moved into the neighborhood like me?"

They looked at each other, each opening his mouth to speak, then snapping it closed. Ayana frowned. Surely it wasn't that big a deal. "Hello? Anyone?"

Reece was the first to speak up. "We had a run in…uh…a difference of opinion about a situation."

"A situation?" She sat her fork down annoyed. "I'm not sure why y'all seem hesitant to tell me how you met, but I don't appreciate the secretive attitude. It's not like I asked you something private. At least I don't think I did." She glared from one to the other.

Reece reached out and took her hand. She resisted his touch, but he held on and laced his fingers with hers. Ayana stared down at her plate. She'd barely eaten a few bites, but her appetite was gone. This was like repeating her past mistakes, and Brooke's comments came back to mind.

"I'm sorry," Reece said. "The truth is when we met it was in the Stecoah-Cheoah Mountain area."

Stecoah-Cheoah sounded familiar to Ayana. She chewed her bottom lip a minute and then snapped her fingers. "That's along the Appalachian Trail when it crosses into North Carolina, right?"

Pleasure washed over Reece's expression, and he grinned. "Exactly right." He nodded in Blaine's direction. "We both enjoy the outdoors and get out that way and other areas around the state where it's less civilized."

"Why doesn't that surprise me?" She smirked. "You both seem a bit I don't know…beastly…in bed."

Reece winked. Blaine seemed uncomfortable, shifting in his chair. Ayana tried not to laugh at him. Reece always called him bear, and it obviously annoyed Blaine. *Yeah*, she thought, *he is like my big bear.*

"Anyway," Reece continued, "we got into a disagreement about what was being done to preserve the wildlife in the area, not allowing rampant hunting. Humans can have tunnel vision regarding things that don't immediately or directly affect them."

"Humans, huh?" She chuckled. "Yeah, I guess you're right. I can't say I've been interested in that kind of thing, but I think it's cool you are." Ayana could have bitten her tongue when she saw the disappointment on Blaine's face. But it cleared. He pushed his plate away and slid back from the table. When he indicated for her to come over to him, she went without hesitation and sat on his lap. His strong arms came around her waist, making her feel secure not for the first time. Reece didn't appear to be bothered by her move. "I can't imagine you two fighting. You get along well."

"That's because we're clear on a few basic facts," Reece commented.

"Like what?"

His eyes swept her with such a possessive look that she shivered and her nipples grew tight. Blaine's hand splayed over her belly, his thumb pointing upward to the space between her breasts. Anticipation of another night spent between these two men took hold of her, and she searched her mind for something to distract the three of them. She wanted to get to know Blaine and Reece, not just jump into bed every time she laid eyes on them.

"So is everyone in your family nature lovers or just you?" she asked Reece.

He continued to stare at her, his attention focused somewhere beneath her eyes, but he answered anyway. "We're all nature lovers. I guess you can say it's in our blood."

Behind her, Blaine grunted in annoyance. Reece chuckled. Ayana rubbed his hand on her belly soothingly, assuming he felt bad sometimes that he had no family. She empathized while not truly understanding what that must feel like. When she looked up at him, his eyes reflected his anger simmering beneath the surface. That's how men were, always disguising their real emotions behind anger.

"You're always teasing Blaine," she chided Reece. "You two are like brothers, and I know that's how brothers act, but it's mean to toss out innuendoes about family when he doesn't have any."

Reece's eyebrows went up, and so did Blaine's. He rushed to say, "It's fine, Ayana. His comments didn't bother me."

"No," she insisted. "It's not all right. I think you owe him an apology, Reece." She sat forward on Blaine's lap to glare at Reece. His expression grew serious, but she wasn't letting it go.

Blaine's face was red with embarrassment. The two of them looked at each other in silence and then her. Blaine opened his mouth to say something else, but clicked his teeth together. Reece sighed and ran a hand through his hair.

"I apologize."

She was surprised to hear sincerity in his tone as he looked at his friend. Then his gaze turned to her. Butterflies danced in her stomach. She was so relieved because she'd thought that if Reece refused, she'd kick him out, and she didn't want to do that.

"The last thing I want to do is offend you, Ayana," Reece said. "Tell me you forgive me."

"I don't know." She'd put her nose in the air and pursed her lips to glower at him. But her anger had melted away as soon as the words tumbled from his lips. She slipped from Blaine's arms, and he let her go, if somewhat reluctantly. She rounded the table and stood in front of Reece. He wasted no time in scooting back to let her climb on his lap facing him. His hands came up her sides and came around to cup her breasts. The squeeze of the small globes followed by a pinch of her nipples made her eyelashes lower and a moan escape her lips. "You can make it up to me," she panted.

"I accept your offer." The heat from his desire was almost palpable. His cock shifted under her, driving her own want to greater proportions. Reece ran a hand over her cheek, and she nuzzled into it. "You are the right one for us. I knew it the first time I saw you in the grocery store."

"For us," she whispered, repeating him. "You were looking for someone to share? Tell me the truth, have you done it before? Shared a woman?" Dizziness assailed her. She should let it go. Somehow she wanted to be important to them, more than any other woman, but at the same time deep inside, she held back. She was looking for a reason to find fault, and she knew it.

Reece looked like he was going to answer, but his cell phone buzzed. He fished it from his pocket, and she watched his dark brows crash low over his eyes on seeing the name on the caller ID. Ayana put her arms over his shoulders and lay on his chest while he answered the call. She paid no attention to his conversation until his voice turned sharp.

"Yeah, we'll be there." He stabbed the disconnect button. "I'm sorry, baby, but we have to go."

Ayana sat up. "What? But I thought y'all were going to stay the night."

He looked really sorry at least. "Something came up. We'll get back as soon as we can."

"We?" She turned to look at Blaine. He was already standing, prepared to go. "As far as I know you two don't work together, so what could have come up? Anything I can help with?"

Reece kissed her. He stood and put her off his lap, cleaning up his place setting. She waited for him to thank her for the offer and explain what the emergency was, but he didn't say a word. Blaine cleaned up his mess as well and then took her into his arms. The kiss he planted on her lips was deeper than what Reece had left her with, but he too didn't give her any explanations. She walked behind them as they headed to the door.

When Reece opened it, he turned. "I promise, we'll come back as soon as we can. I hope we can come over no matter the time."

She took a page from their book and didn't answer the question. "Good night." She shut the door in his face and locked it.

Maybe she was being unreasonable, but the sneaky crap didn't sit well with her. And not answering pissed her off. She stomped back to the kitchen to finish cleaning up from dinner and to load the dishwasher. By the time she was wiping off the table and considering whether she felt like sweeping the floor tonight or in the morning, someone rang her bell. She sighed and glanced at the apple clock over the sink. The night wasn't too far gone, but she had no idea who it could be. She doubted the men were back so soon. When she opened the front door, she grumbled finding Brooke there.

"Oh Lord, woman, really? Give it up. I don't want to hear it," she snapped.

"I have proof!" Brooke shouted just before Ayana could shut the door in her face. Ayana hesitated and swung the door wider. Brooke held up her cell phone. Ayana glared at her.

She sighed. "Fine, come in. If this is nothing, your ass is on my list!"

CHAPTER EIGHT

Brooke stepped into the house and began flipping through something on her phone. She gestured for Ayana to move closer, and Ayana reluctantly did. Brooke explained before she pressed play on what looked like a home video. "I was at a welcome to the neighborhood thing over at Janice's place, and Reece and Blaine were there too. And I saw something that shocked me. I didn't even think. I just recorded it." She laid a hand on Ayana's arm, and Ayana resisted shaking her off. She supposed it was obvious enough she couldn't stand the woman because she was trying to warn her off her two lovers. Not sensing Ayana's annoyance in the least, she chattered on. "You know how there's just always someone with a phone camera or video at the right time?"

Ayana gritted her teeth. "Get on with it."

Brooke sighed and pressed play. When Ayana couldn't see well, she snatched the phone from Brooke to look at it for herself. The scene was in Janice's backyard, or rather at the side of her house. From what she could make out, Brooke was standing just around to the front and aiming her phone at Reece and Blaine.

In front of Blaine was a rake or something, and a thick, deep-colored liquid stained the tool. Blaine was crouched down with his teeth bared in anguish, and his leg had blood running down it. Reece crouched beside him, cursing.

"Fuck, take care of that now before someone sees it," Reece demanded.

Ayana frowned. The man had no patience or concern for Blaine.

The annoyance for his attitude from earlier came flooding back. She pressed pause. "This is it? You're telling me you came over here to show me how Blaine cut his leg?"

Brooke flared her nostrils. "Keep watching."

Ayana pressed play again, and she watched Reece stand up and head off someone who came around the side of the house. Other voices from back there reached her but not clear, so she figured they were toward the other side or maybe inside the woman's house. Reece returned. Brooke zoomed the camera in awkwardly at first catching the bushes. But when she got her focus right, Ayana gasped. Pain tightened her chest. Blaine's cut was more serious than she thought. The gash was wide and deep. He would need stitches without a doubt. Anyone with half a brain could see that.

But when Blaine blew a heavy breath through his nose and held the two sides of his cut together, her head began to swim. The bleeding stopped. Reece brought out a handkerchief and mopped the excess away. Ayana's eyes widened in shock as she watched Blaine's skin begin knitting together.

"What the hell?" she whispered.

"See?" Brooke demanded. "They're not human. At least Blaine isn't. Or maybe they're genetically enhanced like you see in those sci-fi movies."

Ayana couldn't find words to answer. In a few seconds, Blaine's leg had gone from gaping open to healed as if there had never been an injury. The only evidence was a red stain on his sock. He stood up like nothing happened and scooped up the rake. She wondered what he intended to do with it, but then she switched to watching Reece. He sniffed the air.

"Someone's there," he growled.

Behind the camera, she heard Brooke whisper "Damn!" And then the video bounced around the scene until it cut off.

Ayana walked over to her couch and sank onto it. Her breath came out in heavy pants. Her throat was dry, and her stomach ached. "So what happened when it stopped? Did they find you?"

She nodded. Her face was pale like all traces of blood had drained away. The memory of her experience or just rewatching the video must have brought back the fear she'd felt. "Yeah, but not before I emailed myself the video." Her gaze took on an expression of determination. "Blaine or Reece—I don't remember which one—broke my phone. He crushed it like it was nothing, and he said if I ever tell anyone what I saw, I will regret it. I've never told anyone or showed anyone that video. This is the first time, and I thought you should know the truth."

Ayana didn't know what to think. The video had been simple and didn't appear to be doctored. Either way she couldn't deny that Reece and Blaine had a secret they weren't willing to share. All her doubts and fears were magnified by Brooke's video. Of course she would never have thought this.

Confusion clouded her mind. Fear made her jumpy and vulnerable. She thought about them coming back late tonight wanting to be with her. Horrible visions of weird creatures ran through her thoughts, and she closed her eyes and squeezed the bridge of her nose.

"Brooke, can you go now? I'm not in the mood for company."

"Did you see what I showed you?" Brooke yelped. "They're not human, I told you. You can't keep seeing them. Everybody knows you're having an affair with both Reece and Blaine."

Ayana narrowed her eyes at the woman. "Is that what this is about? The fact that I'm seeing both men?"

"No…" Brooke seemed to search for what to say. She dropped her hands to her sides like she was resigned. "Whatever. You do what you want to do. I told you the truth and gave you proof."

She left soon after, and Ayana locked the door behind her. Weary and depressed, she climbed the stairs to her room and took a long bath.

When the bubbles did nothing to soothe her mind, she got out and fell into bed with nothing on. After midnight, still awake, she stiffened when the doorbell rang. Her heart felt like it leaped into her throat. Both longing to see them and scared to, she sat up. While her mind was still a mess, she already knew what she was going to do.

She threw on a robe and descended the stairs as she knotted it. The light outside by the door illuminated Reece's face so she could see him through the peephole. Ayana cleared her throat and swallowed before calling through the door, "Not tonight, Reece."

"Baby, open the door so we can talk. I know you were mad when we left. I want to make it up to you."

She shook her head. Oh her feelings had gone to a whole new level beyond the fact that he hadn't bothered to answer her question about where they were going. Make it up to her? He couldn't begin to, and neither could Blaine. Who'd she been kidding anyway? This thing with the three of them would never have lasted. She wasn't some kind of blind fool who couldn't see the signs—well not now anyway. She'd known that Blaine and Reece had a good sense of smell and hearing from her time spent with them. The oddities she'd observed herself like Blaine's face changing when they were having sex added to what Brooke had showed her. Now, they scared her almost as much as they attracted her. That was the hardest part. She still craved both of them like nobody's business.

"Ayana?" Blaine called through the door.

She rested her forehead on it and closed her eyes. Every time he said her name, something inside reacted. Maybe it was because he didn't say a lot in the first place. When he did, his words had that much more power. And the longing in his tone tonight was unmistakable.

"It's over," she said.

"No, I can't accept that." She thought she picked up hurt in his voice but wouldn't believe it. Blaine wasn't the type. "Open the door,

Ayana. I need to see you face-to-face."

"Hell, no!" she almost shouted and made an effort to get control of herself.

Blaine interrupted. "Did something happen after we left? Do you really want us to keep yelling through the door for all the neighbors to hear at this time of night?"

She ground her teeth. He was right. She didn't want the neighbors in her business. Blaine and Reece hadn't hurt her up until now, so there was no reason to think they would this time. She'd just tell them in their faces she was done and get it over with. Pulling in and blowing out deep breaths, she opened the door. Blaine barged past Reece and dragged her into his arms.

Ayana struggled to free herself. "Blaine, let go. Like I said, it's over. I don't think I want to see you two anymore."

Reece came into the house and shut the door. Her stomach did flip-flops. They were going to make this difficult. She'd had a few difficult break ups with guys in her life. One she'd been so frustrated with over his theatrics, she told the idiot to cry outside. Not the most sensitive, but when she'd had it, she just couldn't deal. This was different. Blaine and Reece were right in so many ways.

Reece turned her in Blaine's arms and stepped close. She found herself sandwiched between them once again with Reece's hands on her cheeks forcing her gently to look up at him. "Is this about us leaving earlier or something else?"

She hesitated. "It's about me, okay? I told you I'm not going to be the slut on the block. I feel like keeping up this relationship is not working for me, so I'm ending it before things go too far and feelings get in the way.

Reece frowned. "It's a little too late for that, don't you think?" She realized he was angry, but there was something deeper behind his eyes. With Reece behind her, she couldn't tell what he was thinking—except for the fact that he hadn't let her go. He was silent holding her too him.

"Don't," he commanded softly against her ear. The word might have been an order, but she sensed pain. Had he fallen for her so quickly? Maybe he'd been through this before. Other women might have gotten involved with them and found out they had secrets they weren't trying to be open about.

She fumbled for words to explain without letting on that she knew more than she should. Reece drew in air through his nose as if he was smelling for something, and then his eyes narrowed. When his lips tightened, she had the feeling he knew Brooke had been there. As far as she could tell, Brooke wasn't wearing perfume or scented lotion that left behind traces of her. Ayana could only smell the bubble bath liquid she'd used earlier.

"What did Brooke say to you?" Reece growled.

Her chest constricted. She stared at the floor. "I don't know what you're talking about. It's late, and I have work in the morning. I think you two should leave."

"Ayana," he began.

Her temper snapped. "What are you going to do, huh? Force me? Is that what you're planning? You're going to rape me if I don't let you stay!" Her words were ballsy but she wasn't feeling it.

Reece's eyes widened. "Of course not. We'd never do that to you. The three of us wanted to be together until tonight. In fact, from the way your body reacted to me earlier, I know you still wanted us before we left. So the question is, what the fuck did Brooke say to you?"

She jabbed an elbow into Blaine's stomach and hurt herself in the process. Blaine rushed to soothe her arm with concern in his expression, but she shook him off. She crossed her arms over her chest. The way her former lovers glanced down at her body, she guessed her robe had inched open a bit struggling to get Blaine off her, but she wouldn't give them the satisfaction of looking down and hiding like she was scared. "I know you didn't just cuss at me, Reece."

"I'm sorry—"

"Save it," she bit out. "I told you I want you both out. Now!"

Reece appeared ready to argue but then changed his mind. She let out a sigh of relief when he turned toward the door. "Let's go, Blaine." Blaine didn't move, but Reece made a low sound like a warning in his throat. Blaine followed him out the door, and Ayana slammed it closed before locking it with both locks and a chain.

She sagged against the door. Tears fell down her cheeks. *Why, why why? Why can't I have someone special in my life long-term? Why couldn't I have had them?*

Sniffling, she turned off the lights and went back up to her bed to toss and turn the rest of the night.

* * * *

Ayana woke up late the next morning after falling asleep around five thirty. Her head hurt, and her stomach growled since she hadn't finished her dinner the night before. After brushing her teeth and dressing, she went downstairs to make coffee. Maybe then she could see her way clear to do some work. What she really wanted to do was feel sorry for herself and take a couple of Tylenol PMs to knock her ass out the rest of the day.

On the way back from the kitchen, she thought she saw a cop car parked across the street. She walked to the front door and opened it to mayhem. Two police cars were parked in front of Brooke's house, and one had pulled into her driveway.

Ayana's heart hammered in her chest as she scanned the street for immediate danger, and when she didn't see anything she stepped outside. Brooke in a scanty nightie clung to the arm of one of the officers who looked harassed in the middle of taking her statement.

Neighbors dotted the street, each craning their necks to listen to every detail Brooke was telling the police.

"Didn't you hear me?" she shouted. "I know who did it. What are you going to do about it? They broke into my house and smashed everything—the TV, my glass dining room table—*everything*!"

Dramatic much? Ayana sighed at the way the woman behaved. While she felt bad for Brooke, she didn't think it took wrapping herself around the man and sobbing as loud as she was to be sure everyone heard her. Brooke must have sensed Ayana had joined the spectators. She spun around to glare at Ayana and then ran over to her on bare feet. Ayana frowned. If she was going to start something, she better know the police being there wasn't going to stop Ayana from defending herself. She took a protective stance and waited until Brooke drew up in front of her.

"This is your fault," she spat. "You told them, didn't you?"

Ayana's eyes widened. "Excuse me?"

"You heard me. I know you told Blaine and Reece about what I told you, and they broke into my house last night and destroyed the place. All I could do was hide in a closet and pray for help! I couldn't even get to my cell phone, I was so terrified." She whirled between Ayana and the police she'd left standing in front of her house. "I want them arrested. I am pressing charges."

She continued to rant, but Ayana was no longer listening. Was she right? Had the two men left her place only to go over and get revenge on Brooke? Reece had somehow known that Brooke had been at her place last night, and she could see the anger in his eyes when he demanded to know what Brooke said. The woman had claimed Reece and Blaine threatened her if she ever let their secret out. Was Ayana that much of a poor judge of character that she didn't know these men were capable of traumatizing a single woman, of destroying her property because she showed a video of them?

"Why aren't you going over there to arrest them?" Brooke yelled, capturing Ayana's attention again. She pointed toward Blaine's house, and Ayana turned to look. Blaine's truck wasn't there. The officer walked over to Reece's house where his SUV was parked in the drive. He knocked, and it seemed that the entire block including Ayana waited on baited breath to see if he would answer. After several pounds on the door, no one came. Brooke hugged herself and shivered visibly. "I can't stay here. I'm going to stay with my parents."

With that announcement, she marched back across the street. Ayana wasn't surprised to find that she commandeered another officer to come with her inside the house because she was "too scared to go by herself." The two women Ayana had met on the first day sidled up to her shaking their heads.

"I suspect this is a scheme of Brooke's to get her parents to pay her bills," one of the women said.

Ayana made a noncommittal sound. The woman needed no more than that to continue gossiping.

"She couldn't find a man to pay them for her, so she cooked up this idea as an excuse to go back to living off her folks. They've got money, and Brooke has never been the same since her divorce. Guess she loved that guy a lot, but he ran off with a woman half his age."

"Hmm," the other neighbor chimed in, "either that or she loved *his* money. Alimony only lasts but so long."

Ayana excused herself. She didn't want to deal with Brooke's mess. Whether it was a ploy or not, she didn't know. Hell, she knew people did desperate things when it came to money even when they could just be straightforward about it. Her family had once accused her aunt of a plot when she claimed a man had climbed her fire escape, broke into her apartment, and raped her. Ayana thought it was horrifying that her own family wouldn't believe her, but her aunt was so wild normally, one couldn't put anything past her. Everyone thought she'd done it to avoid paying the rent.

Either way, none of it changed her situation with Blaine and Reece. She headed back up the walk to her door. Behind her, she heard Brooke's chatter as she exited her house. Someone said, "Who is that?" and Ayana couldn't help looking to see.

Would the drama never end? Brooke stopped cold at the end of her driveway, eyes wide as the third officer, who had driven off in a hurry while she was out acting a fool in the middle of the street, returned with a man cuffed in his back seat. Apparently, Brooke knew him from the look on her face.

She put a hand up to her mouth. "Cal?"

The man sneered at her. Against her better judgment, Ayana scooted back to the end of the drive to hear better what was being said. The officer asked Brooke, "What connection do you have to this man, Miss James?"

Brooke's face went red but she didn't say a word. The man must have heard what the officer asked, because he started yelling. "I'll tell you. That bitch showed up at my house after we had some fun together. She's the cause of me losing everything. My wife took the kids. She's gone. You satisfied, you slut?"

Brooke started crying. Despite what she'd done, Ayana felt sorry for the woman. To be called on the kind of life she led right to her face and in front of everyone must be humiliating. "I-I-I," she stuttered. "I have to get out of here."

A minivan pulled up then, and Brooke ran to it even before the old man behind the wheel pulled to a complete stop. The officer yelled for her to wait, but she jumped in and shook the driver's arm mouthing something to him Ayana couldn't hear. The old man calmly threw the minivan in reverse and eased out of the fray. The officers shook their heads. Ayana imagined they weren't about to give her crazy tail a chase. They'd catch up with her later. Ayana could guess now just like she supposed everyone else did about what happened. Brooke thought she could get one of her lovers to leave his wife for her. When he didn't, she thought she'd cause trouble by going to his house. His grief at losing his family made him retaliate on her. Now he was even more screwed getting arrested for breaking and entering and destruction of private property.

"Well," one of the neighbors said, "Lawnwood Drive is not a dull place. I'll give you that."

"Amen," another replied.

Ayana hurried inside her house and shut the door behind her. Blaine and Reece were innocent of this crime, but where were they? *What* were they? She hated more than anything that she still missed them. *I might be an even bigger idiot than Brooke.*

CHAPTER NINE

Days had passed, almost a week, and Ayana had caught a glimpse of Reece coming and going from his house, but she hadn't seen Blaine. His truck was now parked in his driveway, but it had been Reece who returned it, and Blaine hadn't been with him. She wondered where he was and what he was doing. She ached when she caught sight of Reece. He'd stopped outside his house and stared in her direction where she hid peeking through the blinds. She didn't think he saw her, but such an intense look of longing had come over his expression, it shook her. She'd stumbled away from the window, confused and depressed.

She puttered around the house, made herself some lunch, and then went back to work. Her productivity was way down, but Kevin hadn't complained as yet. She knew it was a matter of time though. He'd demand she either talk about what her issue was or get over it and do what he hired her to do. Kevin didn't pull any punches, and she was okay with that.

Around six in the evening, someone pounded on her door. At her desk on the second floor, her heart began to beat in cadence. Brooke hadn't been seen since the day of the break-in, so it wasn't likely to be her. No one else visited, not since she'd shown herself to be less than eager for the whole gossiping thing. Figuring she better see who it was only to get some peace, she went downstairs. Reece's handsome face met hers through the peephole, and she began to shake. Not from fear—or not from fear *alone*—but from missing him.

She opened the door. He stood there saying nothing, just looking at her. She stared back, taking in his unshaven appearance, his eyes red as if he hadn't slept the last week. Even with wrinkled clothes and tired, he was sexy as hell. "I need to talk to you, Ayana. May I come in?"

She hesitated. "I don't know."

"I want to tell you everything—about me and Blaine."

She gasped and then stepped back to let him pass. Healing fast like she'd seen in the video was nothing he was going to pass off as a trick of the camera or slight of hand. He better come with something real, or she'd kick him out on his ass. Funny enough as she followed him to the couch in her living room, she prayed he would give her a good excuse, anything that would allow her to let him back into her life. Him and Blaine.

She stayed on her feet in case she had to jet, but it was everything she could do not to go over and sit on his lap when he sat down. She folded her arms over her chest and leaned against the side of the stairs to keep herself in place. Glancing at Reece through her lashes, she noticed he seemed just as hungry to get close to her. He laced his fingers together and rested his elbows on his thighs.

"What I'm going to say will be hard for you to believe. Even that bi…Brooke doesn't know this about Blaine and me. It's not the kind of thing we ever tell anyone who is not like us."

"Like you?" Her stomach flip-flopped. "What do you mean like you?"

He continued as if she hadn't spoken. "The reason I'm telling you is because I care about you—deeply. So does Blaine."

"Hm, funny, if he cares so much why isn't he here too?"

"Because I care," he said, pinning her in place with those eyes that could look deep inside her and know what she longed for, "I know you're the one for us. We both knew it the day we met, but we didn't want to scare you."

She blinked at him.

He sighed and leaned back to run his hands through his hair. "I think I should show you. Don't be scared. Please, Ayana, not for a million years would I ever hurt you."

She watched him move her coffee table into the doorway between the living room and the kitchen. He glanced around as if to judge the space. Ayana worried her bottom lip. What the heck was he about to do?

Her eyes bugged almost painfully when he began taking his clothes off. "Uh, dude, what do you think you're doing?" she demanded.

Despite his seriousness earlier, he smiled and winked. "You missed my naked body, didn't you?"

That goes without saying.

"I don't want to rip apart my clothes and maybe have to slough home naked if you reject me." Although he joked, she heard the emotion behind his words. Whatever she said, how ever she reacted to what he was about to show her, Reece would be hurt if she turned him away. This could be all an act, him saying he cared, but she believed him. She admitted to herself that she *wanted* to believe him which made it that much more difficult.

He watched her face, an expression of tenderness in his until it began to change. Ayana gave a sharp cry when his nose grew out like a snout, and his eyes stretched farther apart. His entire being enlarged, and hair sprouted from seemingly every pore. Ayana knew why he'd needed the space because all of a sudden a frickin' nine hundred-pound brown bear, give or take, filled her living room.

She threw herself against the stairs, fingers hurting from gripping the spokes so tightly. The bear took a few steps toward her, and she bit off a tiny scream. He stopped, eyeing her with small round brown eyes. Ayana's throat dried. She was too scared to move. Because she just wasn't scared enough, her stupid gaze landed on the bear's paws. Long and thick claws curved into her carpet. One swipe could cut her to ribbons.

She licked her lips. "Please…"

His head went down like he was ashamed, and he began to shrink. The hair receded, muscles and bone taking on the shape of a man. Soon Reece knelt on the floor just as naked as when he started. He didn't move, didn't threaten her in any way.

"You're," she began.

He nodded.

"Are you a man who can turn into a bear, or a bear who can turn into a man?"

He cast her a confused look. "I believe I am equally both, as is Blaine."

She sank to the floor, her limbs no longer able to hold her. What she should be doing was hightailing it out of there, but somehow she didn't want to go. "Tell me."

He stood and moved as if to come closer, but she held up her hand. He respected her wish to keep distance between them and went to put his clothes back on. She watched his every move, fascinated by his body and what he could do. Sure, it still scared the crap out of her, and she didn't know if she should be grossed out that she'd essentially had sex with an animal. But this was still Reece, the man that made her laugh and knew just how to touch her. He enjoyed cuddling, and he loved her food. Now she knew why their appetites were so huge. Who could afford to feed a bear every day?

"How long have you been like this? Did someone experiment on you?"

He laughed. "No, I was born this way, and so were most of my brothers and sisters. Some carry the gene but never change. We don't know why. The day I met Blaine, I knew he was like me. I could sense it. But he's a black bear."

Her eyes widened in awe. A black bear. Was he bigger than Reece when he changed? She guessed he was. Blaine was built like a powerhouse. A shiver of fear rippled over her skin.

Reece took his seat on the couch and glanced at her before looking away. "Another thing that will be hard for you to accept."

Ayana ran a hand over her face. "More? I don't know if I've accepted what I just saw with my own eyes. That bear terrifies me. I want you to go, but I want you to stay. I'm scared and confused. I don't want any of this to be true, but I don't think I can take anymore." Without warning, she started to cry and scrubbed an arm over her eyes. "Stupid. I hate crying in front of others. I never…" She sobbed to her shame.

Reece got up and walked over to draw her into his arms. Ayana resisted, but she was all out of strength. He picked her up and carried her to the couch to sit her on his lap. She tried to resist sinking against chest but failed. His scent was all man, nothing even hinting at a wild beast. His skin was warm and taut across solid muscle. She pressed her lips to the pulse at his throat and closed her eyes. From head to toe she shook and couldn't stop.

Reece held her close and stroked her back all the while crooning something to her she couldn't quite hear. The tone of his voice soothed her frazzled mind to a degree. Her hands crept up around his neck, and she pressed against his chest.

"What's the other thing you have to say?"

"We—our kind—have certain people that are meant to be our mates. Unlike humans, we don't have divorce. We choose someone, and that's it forever."

She lifted her head and stared at him. "No divorce. Like none at all?"

He shook his head.

"Weird. But aren't male bears like polygamous?"

He grinned. "Do you know that from study, or are you guessing?"

She flared her nostrils at him. "Answer the question. If—and that is a huge, *huge* if—if I accept you for what you are, I'm not going for the I have an excuse to cheat, baby. Bears have more than one mate!"

"Remember I said I believe we are wholly bear and wholly human. We are different from humans in that we can shape-shift and different from bears obviously in that we can reason as men even taking a bear's form. Fate has sorted out how we mate and with whom. If Blaine and I had been simple bears, when we met you, we would have fought even as long as a month to see who was the more powerful Alpha male who earned the right to mate with you first."

She rolled her eyes and tried getting off his lap, but he held on. "I don't appreciate being looked at as if I'm nothing but a body."

"Baby, I promise you, you are much more than that for both of us. We are not just bears. We knew you were our mate, destined to be ours. The circumstances are rare but not unheard of. Oddly enough in the same way that I'm sure you are mine, I'm sure you are Blaine's. That's why we never fought and why we will never look at another woman."

His words didn't instill a lot of confidence. Sure, a warm, fuzzy feeling came over her having two sexy men claim her, but the terminology—their mate? Theirs? She frowned at him. "I don't know. I've never gone in for the destined thing. I think there are many people we could end up with and be happy together, but that *one*, a soul mate?" She wrinkled her nose. "Sounds too orchestrated. And shoot, women outnumber men. How greedy could I get snagging up both of you? It's too good to be true."

He pulled her back to his chest and wrapped his arms around her waist. His face alongside hers with little kisses planted on her skin sent tremors coursing through her body. His breath warmed her. "Baby, tell me how it could be that Blaine and I are what we are."

She squirmed. "How should I know?"

"If there could be shape-shifters like Blaine and I and my family, and as you can see that's not too good to be true, then it stands to reason anything else regarding us is possible. It's possible that there's one person that can complete us. And it's also possible you are that one."

Her mind refused to accept it even though her heart beat faster with excitement. Leaning on the belief that this was meant to be felt kind of good. She wanted to go with what he said, but she wasn't quite ready. "When you left that night and didn't tell me where you were going…"

"A family member was in a fight. I'm sorry. I could hardly admit that we were leaving civilization for a bit."

She blinked at him over her shoulder. "You're telling me it was a fight between…" She swallowed. "It was an animal fight?'

He nodded. Ayana shivered. She settled into his chest again clenching her fists against the tops of her thighs. Whatever she'd felt she had accepted a minute ago, flew out the window. Them shifting into beasts and going at it head-to-head with other animals was too much. A woman had concerns like another woman turning her man's head or work taking too much of his time, but this was crazy.

She pressed the heels of her hands to her eyes and drew in sharp breaths then blew them out. Nothing worked to calm her. "I don't know about this, Reece. I-I like you a lot. I don't want to let you go."

"Then don't."

She started to protest, but he covered her mouth. His hand slid down her front to press gently against her mound. A shiver chilled her bringing goose bumps to her skin. Reece squeezed between her legs, and she moaned, arching her hips toward his hand. She rested both her hands over his to stop his movement. "Maybe we shouldn't."

"Why not?" He pushed her hand aside and lowered the zipper on her shorts. She didn't get a squeak past her lips before he'd reached inside and inched around her panty line to finger her clit. Ayana gasped. Her head fell onto Reece's shoulder.

"Reece," she breathed.

"Hmm?" He added more fingers to his gentle massage. Her bud

swelled at his touch, and he pinched it. Ayana's ass came up off his lap, but he held her in place while rubbing her. She was so wet so fast. She drew her bottom lip between her teeth and shut her eyes. Reece teased her mouth with the tip of his tongue until she parted her lips. He invaded, filling her mouth just as he pushed digits deep within her wet snatch. After a few moments, he drew back. "Aw, baby, you've been neglected this week, haven't you?"

She keened, fighting her attraction to him, but nothing could stop how hot she was. And when Reece tugged her shorts off her hips and lowered them down her legs, she didn't give much of a fight. Her panties soon followed the shorts to the floor. Reece slid out from under her and turned her to lie on the couch. He knelt so that his head was between her thighs. She caught her breath.

"Reece, I don't know—"

He squeezed one of her thighs and raised it. "Do you have any idea how much I've missed touching your smooth cocoa skin? Do you know how I've longed to taste you?" He didn't wait for her to answer but delved between her legs to give her pussy a swipe. She writhed under him.

She put her hand on his shoulder, torn. The question she wanted to ask didn't fall from her lips. She didn't know how he'd react and didn't want to hurt him. Her mind spun when he gave several swipes along her slit and then drove his tongue deep into her creamy entrance. For an instant, she rode his mouth, fast losing control.

He raised his head. "Don't worry, baby. I'm going to make you come once just to ease your need, and then we will go get Blaine."

Her mouth dropped open. "How did you know?"

"Because as I said, just as I know you are mine, I know you're his too. It's hurting you to be away from him. Trust me, he needs you too."

She looked away from him. "I'm not sure of my feelings."

"You will be. I have faith. Now then where were we?" His eyes sparked with lust. The man was willing to knock the edge off her desire, but he must be ready to explode. She couldn't help noticing the strain in the front of his jeans and recalled how much she enjoyed his cock. She wanted it in her now, but he was right, she'd been worrying about Blaine. Was it genuine hurt that she felt with him gone? Or just lust for her second lover? She wasn't even positive yet if she could move past the fact that they were shape-shifting bears, for Pete's sake.

The second Reece started lapping at her clit, running his tongue across the sensitive bud in a rhythmic dance, she forgot everything else. She whined and groaned, raising her hips to meet his mouth. Her orgasm escalated until she was at the precipice.

"Yes, oh, yes," she cried, encouraging him. "More, Reece. Don't stop!"

He gripped her thighs on both sides until it hurt, but she rode his mouth faster. He closed his lips over her clit and sucked hard. She screamed in ecstasy. The orgasm was so powerful it drove her to sit up with him still on her. She held onto the back of the couch and tangled her fingers in his hair while she pumped against his face. Reece didn't let up until the aftershocks rocked her body, and she fell back down.

Panting, eyes slitted, she watched him rise and wipe his mouth. Now she saw the slight change she'd seen that first night. Reece's eyes were still russet brown, but shaped slightly different. Danger lurked in the depths, but she was less afraid.

"Now," he said in a voice that was gravely and unlike his own, "you get cleaned up so we can bring Blaine home."

"Yes, the sooner, the better."

CHAPTER TEN

The ride out to where Blaine was took an hour and a half. All Ayana saw on both sides of the street at one point were trees and more trees. At least between them the sun had less opportunity to bake her during this early summer, but what the heck was she going to do if they wanted her to spend time out here. She was a city girl through and through.

"Where is he?" she asked. "Why couldn't you have just called him?"

Reece hesitated. He reached across to take her hand in his, and she let him thread his fingers between hers. "I don't know if you've noticed, but Blaine is a bit wilder than I am. He is influenced more by his animal instincts."

"Uh, yeah, I think I noticed that. Are you saying he's lost in the woods?" Trepidation kicked up her heart beat.

"No, not lost." He turned his attention to the winding road. "We have an area out there where we stay. I'd say it's halfway between civilized and living in the wild. Just a plot of land to get away from it all. Members of my family use it most of the time, and periodically when Blaine and I feel the need to stretch our legs, we drive out."

Ayana said nothing. She looked out her window as he spoke. For the second time since she knew the truth about them, she felt separated. "So he's there?"

"More or less," he responded. "Blaine sometimes goes off alone. He leaves everything that ties him to the city and humans at the area I mentioned, and he goes off. He doesn't return until he's ready. Usually that happens when something is bugging him."

"Meaning me this time, right?"

He lifted and kissed her fingers. "This isn't your fault, baby."

"But if I hadn't broken it off he wouldn't have needed to leave. Why do I have the feeling he's been out of touch longer than normal?" Reece said nothing. She chewed her lip. "You can track him, right? You can like sniff him out?"

He grinned. "More bear facts?"

She stuck her tongue out at him and rolled her eyes.

Reece pulled the SUV onto a well-worn dirt road between the trees. He stopped outside of a large cabin that looked like it could certainly house his family and more. A young boy chased another one across the opening and into the trees. She wondered if they shifted into bear cubs.

Her lover came around and helped her out of the vehicle. He kept his arm about her waist as they walked toward the cabin. "For your information," he said, "a bear can smell up to twenty miles. Pretty useful. But we're not going to hunt Blaine down. He's coming to us. That's why you're here. So wiggle your sexy little ass to get your scent going."

Her eyes widened when he smacked her on the butt. "Really?"

He burst out laughing. "No, he'll smell you here whether you move or not." Reece tapped the side of his nose. "Good for tracking down food, wandering cubs—and mates."

She followed him into the cabin not knowing what to think. The loud debating among the inhabitants of the cabin came to an abrupt halt as soon as she stepped inside. If what Reece had told her was true, his family already knew they were coming. To act like they were shocked annoyed her. The sharp eyes of an older couple, a middle aged couple, and various other men and women nearer to her age stared at her. At that moment Ayana remembered that many of them could shape-shift into bears. She had visions of them ripping her limb from limb, and she bolted around Reece to run for her life.

He caught her and held her in his strong arms. Gentle words poured into her ears, but she couldn't hear him beyond the blood rushing there. Her heart beat so fast it hurt. Not until the old woman put a small, soft hand in hers did she calm down.

"It's okay, dear. You don't have to be afraid. I'm Granny." She grinned showing a gap on the top right side of her smile. Somehow that and her wispy gray hair and tiny frame struck Ayana as comical. Her fears ebbed even more.

"Hello, Granny," she said. As much family as she had herself, both her maternal and paternal grandmothers had passed before she was born. "I'm Ayana."

"Beautiful name," someone else chipped in.

Ayana turned to face them. Reece kept his arms wrapped around her and held her back against his chest. "This is my and Blaine's mate, Ayana. I'm sure you'll welcome her to the family?"

If she wondered about Alpha attitude before, she knew right away Reece was it and no doubt Blaine too. Reece might have raised his voice on his statement's end, but it was far from a question. His words had been a command. Heads bobbed yes all around. No one questioned, at least in her presence, who he thought he was taking a human as a mate or in being fine with sharing her with Blaine. For all she knew if they didn't mate outside the family, they'd have to inbreed. *Ew!*

While Reece introduced her all around the family, including his parents and his grandfather, the door opened. Another woman walked in. This one was drop-dead gorgeous with thick black hair that extended down to her butt. She was small built with big boobs and a tiny waist. The only flaw Ayana saw—or it could have been an asset to a man—was the fact that her eyes were creepily almost black. She was an exotic beauty. The woman was dressed scantily with a tube top covering her breasts and a miniskirt that looked more like a strip of cloth, covering her lower parts. "We're back," she announced as if she needed to for anyone but Ayana.

Ayana couldn't help but look up at Reece to see his reaction to the woman. Her lover's lips had tightened, and his eyes narrowed. She wondered why he wasn't pleased to see her. She should have been happy that he had that reaction and not one of lust. His reasons for being irritated became all too clear when Blaine walked in right behind the woman. If Ayana's heart had been pounding earlier, it felt like it stopped then. In the few days since she last saw Blaine, she'd somehow lost touch with how stocky and sexy he was. His muscles strained against any material that had the nerve to cover his perfect body. Not that he had on much. He'd apparently drawn on a pair a sweatpants, which hung low on his lean hips, and he carried a T-shirt in his hand. His feet were bare. Come to think of it, so were the woman's.

She remembered how Reece had needed to remove his clothes to shift if he didn't want to ruin them. Reece had said Blaine was out in the wild in bear form. He'd gotten back quick. She expected him to take his time, but then if he could smell twenty miles, than he might have picked up that she was coming long before now. But what concerned her was this woman. She'd come back with him. Reece had told her Blaine went off alone when he was in a funk. She couldn't blame him since she'd broken it off, but damn the man anyway.

Ayana went to move, but Reece kept her where she was. She gritted her teeth staring between Blaine and the woman. Reece lowered his face next to hers, covering his words with a kiss to her cheek. "Easy, baby."

"Who is she?" she bit out low.

"My cousin." He answered the unspoken questions she had. "No relation to him, but she wants him for her mate."

Blaine's dark eyes shifted to her. They seemed to burn her skin. She couldn't tell if the look he had was one of anger or desire, or both. Energy rolled off of him in her direction making her short of breath. He didn't move from his spot near the door, nor did he call her to him. But he never took his gaze from her face.

Resolved to go to him, Ayana took a step out of Reece's arms. This time he let her go. Before she could get very far, the woman moved in front of her, blocking her vision of Blaine. A wide insincere grin spread over her beautiful face. She held out a hand. "Hi, I'm Gwen. You're my cousin Reece's mate, right?"

Ayana's eyebrows went up. From years of practice she did her best to wither Gwen with a look from head to toe. Then she moved around her to go to Blaine. She stopped inches from him. He towered over her, that big chest looking so lickable. He still held the shirt clutched in a large fist at his side. With boldness she didn't feel, Ayana laid her hand on the center of his chest, and unless she was mistaken, he flinched like she'd burned him.

He didn't say a word, and neither did she. The entire room had gone silent again. At least she knew now they were just nosey as hell and it wasn't about her being human when she walked in. Blaine took her hand and pulled her outside. She heard Gwen protest, and from the heavy footsteps behind her, she figured Reece followed.

They walked off the porch and into the trees a ways. Blaine stopped at a particularly old one where the trunk had bent so low it formed a chair. He gestured as if he wanted her to sit, but she ignored it. She put her hands on her hips facing him. "You were out with that woman?"

I should calm down and not get an attitude. What right do I have to get pissed off at him? I broke things off. He had every right to see whoever he wanted to see. Please tell me they haven't been together all this time.

"No," he said. What the heck did that mean?

Reece beside them opened his mouth to speak, but she held up a hand. He fell silent. "I don't want to hear it from Reece. I want to hear it from you, Blaine. You don't owe me an explanation at all, but…" She licked her lips and willed herself not to cry or beg. Had she said she liked them? *Like* was so not the word with all this emotion.

"I was out alone as I always am when I'm upset," he responded. "She looked for me as she always does. She found me only as I was coming back when I smelled you."

She reached up to run her fingers over his cheek. His jaw was so unyielding, so strong and male. Like Reece he hadn't shaved in a while. "Have the two of you ever—don't answer that!"

She looked at the ground, but he lifted her chin and kissed her. "No, never. And we never will. You are my mate."

Ayana didn't pretend to get this mating stuff, but Blaine looked even surer of that fact than Reece. She knew looking into his eyes that it had messed him up thinking he'd lost her. How could he be that into her that fast? Was it really built into their makeup, the person they were meant to be with forever? Blaine and Reece appeared to be convinced it was.

Blaine didn't ask her if they were all back together. He assumed she was when he hoisted her onto his lap as he sat on the tree. Her legs hung over his thighs as she faced him with her arms around his neck. She let herself be consumed by his hungry kisses. When they were both out of breath, Blaine released her swollen numb lips. "I have to have all of you, Ayana. I have to touch you without these clothes."

He tugged at her blouse as if he was just short of ripping it from her flesh. Ayana squeaked and pushed his hands away. "Let me do it."

She leaned back and crossed her arms to pull her shirt over her head. Blaine's eyes shifted a little at the sight of her breasts still half hidden behind her bra. He cupped them, and she yelped when he ripped the bra apart like it was paper. "Blaine!"

"You don't need that. You have your shirt." His expression showed no apology whatsoever as he dropped her bra on the ground.

Ayana looked around for Reece, and he stood behind her, his stare riveted to her body as Blaine exposed her. She wanted them both so much, she didn't care they were within walking distance from the cabin.

If her mind was clearer, she'd realize that every member of Reece's family probably knew what they were up to. But damn it had been days since they'd been together. She was getting hers.

Blaine ran his hands up and down her thighs. She wriggled off his lap to take her own skirt off before he could destroy it. She let the denim material fall and followed it with her panties. Blaine's eyes blazed. He ran his tongue over his bottom lip, and looked like he was going to drop to his knees. The man loved eating her out like nobody she knew, but she stopped him with a hand in the middle of his chest.

She leaned in and kissed his lips just as she felt Reece gliding his palms over her ass. He squeezed each cheek and delved between them to massage her anus with his finger. She moaned arching her back. Reece stepped closer. He rested a hand on her hip and rubbed her rear entry faster. She dug her nails into Blaine's shoulders and broke the kiss. Her lips parted in a gasp as she closed her eyes and put her head back.

"Mm, that feels so good," she murmured.

Not to be outdone, Blaine reached between her legs and pushed his fingers into her pussy. She almost wept at the pleasure. Her legs trembled, and she would have collapsed if Blaine hadn't added support to her other hip. They were just using their fingers in the front and back, and yet, she was going to come.

She held onto Blaine tighter and hoisted a knee onto his thigh. Here she was in the middle of the woods, between two sexy men who were fully clothed while she was stark naked. She didn't care. This felt too good to get all shy and nervous about who would see. For the moment, she felt just as feral as her men were.

They didn't let up in their attacks on her body. She could only hold onto Blaine and ride it out. Their fingers stroked and pumped, wrenching every sensation of bliss in her core. She panted and cried out. Her voice echoed for miles. She squirmed between them, and then she screamed. Her orgasm erupted, making her sag into Blaine.

"You're so wet," her stocky lover murmured as if in awe.

Reece tugged her from his arms and turned her. "Let me wet myself with you, baby."

She didn't question him, knowing what he planned. With acceptance and excitement, she watched him unbutton his pants and lower the zipper. He pushed his boxers aside to let his cock loose. She bit her bottom lip. Reece was so turned on, he didn't waist time. He gripped her around the waist and jerked her up. His hard shaft impaled her. She gasped. He pushed as far as he could go, holding her up like she weighed nothing. Crushing her against his chest, he ground in and out of her, rough and good.

Her forehead dropped onto his shoulder. He finished and then set her down facing Blaine. By this time, he'd opened his pants too and settled better on the tree so he could have back support while he took her weight. Reece raised her again, this time to rest her in Blaine's arms. Ayana arched her hips to lower down on Blaine's cock. He growled low in his throat.

"Easy," Reece snapped.

Blaine gentled his hold on her and held her still while Reece swung his leg over the narrow tree trunk. He stepped closer to her from behind. Ayana grabbed her ass cheek and pulled one side apart for him. She watched in anticipation as Reece guided his rod to her anus. She couldn't help shouting "Yes!" when his cock head popped past her barrier.

Both men gritted their teeth, hissing like they were close to blowing. They'd better not. "I want it until I can't bear it anymore. You know how I like it Blaine, Reece," she demanded.

At her sass, Blaine smacked her ass cheek. She moaned.

Blaine moved her up and down his cock, and soon Reece matched the rhythm. Together, they pounded into her from both ways. Ayana bounced on Blaine's lap while she watched Reece's shaft disappear inside her from the back. Her lovers grunted their enjoyment, neither one of them looking up from her slender form. She'd always thought she wasn't that much to look at which was why she tried showing it off a bit more to look sexy. But Blaine and Reece looked at her like she was a supermodel, one that had been given to them alone as a present.

Blaine tugged lightly on her hair to make her put her head back. When she did, he covered her mouth. His tongue slipped between her lips, and she surrendered to him, allowing him to explore her warm depths. She swirled her tongue with his until Blaine demanded attention as well. He reached out and took hold of her chin to turn her head. Reece released her mouth, and Blaine claimed it. His kisses were rougher, more insistent. His tongue filled up her mouth so much she sucked on it, and he groaned.

They pushed into her until she was weak and sore. She'd come half a dozen times. Blaine had come once, yet he never stopped. His cock was rigid inside of her. Reece didn't let off, but when he was ready, he pushed her toward Blaine's chest. Blaine hugged her to him. The two of them stilled. Reece pounded into her ass, squeezing her hips. His muscles were all tight and glistened in the sunlight that reached them between the trees. He shouted her name. His warmth filled her rear.

Panting for breath, he pulled out. She rested her head on Blaine's shoulder. His body jerked, but he pulled out of her and held her close. She knew he had reached a second orgasm, but she also recognized he'd have to force himself to be gentle. She'd have to grow stronger if she was going to be Blaine's lover long-term.

Behind her, Reece stroked her head. "Are you okay?"

"Yeah." She had her eyes closed and didn't have the energy yet to get up.

The tree trunk sagged a little. "Give her to me," Reece said. "Her thighs are probably aching from being stretched across you so long." She sighed. Her heart swelled while Blaine handed her over like precious cargo.

Still they didn't argue, except for that small something when Reece had reminded Blaine to be gentler with her. How could they be so convinced when she was so scared? Anyway, now that her lust had been sated, she remembered that they had to go back to the cabin. All those nosey folk would be looking at her, knowing she'd just jumped not one but two men in the woods like a slut. *Great.*

After some time, Reece set her on her feet. "Come on. We should get back. It's getting late."

Ayana sighed again. Well, time to face the music. They walked the way they came with her in the middle and the two men on both sides of her. If she didn't know anything, she knew that this relationship was not natural. Not natural at all, and she might not ever get used to it.

CHAPTER ELEVEN

Blaine had been silent all night. Ayana kept waiting for him to say something, to discuss her dismissal of them or to have him demand to know what she wanted to do, but he just sat there at her side. And it wasn't like she thought he was at peace or accepting either. She didn't know how she knew, but she was sure Blaine was furious. He fairly bristled with it, and her suspicions were proven right by the way Reece's family—including Gwen—tiptoed on eggshells around him.

She touched his arm and looked at him, waiting for him to meet her eyes, but he stubbornly kept his head down. Hurt even though she had no right to be, she opened her mouth to say something to him. Someone else grabbed her hand, and she glanced up to find it was Reece's mother.

"Come on and dance with us," she invited.

Ayana couldn't help her lips curling up and drawing back at bit. "Uh, yeah, I don't really do the dance around the fire thing."

The woman wouldn't take no for an answer. She kept a huge smile on her face while pulling Ayana onto her feet. Embarrassed, Ayana scanned the scene around her. The family had elected to barbecue outside. They had huge spits going with meat covering every spot. At least they cooked it, she thought, considering they were half animal.

There were more people around the tables and fire now, some of which she suspected had come in from the woods. A man at the edge of the group flipped the switch on a CD player, and music filled the air. For some reason, she'd thought they'd be playing the banjo or a harmonica or something. White boy music is what she called it, but the beat wasn't bad.

Reece's mother dragged her to the line of women who were dancing in the middle of the group. They shook their hips and stomped their feet. Most of them were barefoot. Ayana tossed a meaningful look toward Reece, but he only raised his beer and grinned. She rolled her eyes at him and tried catching Blaine's eye. He didn't look at her. Her heart sank. Why wouldn't he look at her? They'd just had sex in the woods for Pete's sake. She knew he wasn't regretting it. She didn't. But all she could think about was what would happen when they got back to the city.

"Dance for them," the older woman commanded.

Ayana decided she wasn't getting away without a least an attempt, so she moved in her own way. Soon she got into it and knew she was showing those women a thing or two about how it was done. Her sandals hindered her movements, so she kicked them off, raised her arms, and gyrated over to Reece barefoot. When she spun around, dipped to touch the ground, and came up slowly with her ass in his face, the man looked like he was about to drool. She laughed snapping her fingers to the music.

By that time, Blaine was looking too. She danced over to him and pushed her fingers through his thick dark hair. In the firelight, his eyes grew darker, but she wasn't the least bit afraid. She shimmied in front of him, this time capturing his stare. His desire for her was plain and so much more. He loved her. There was no mistake about it. The knowledge terrified her, and she pivoted on her heel to return to the women.

When the song blended into another, some of the men jumped up and joined in. One particular man, tall and cute—although nowhere near as sexy as her lovers—danced over to her. He put a hand out to take hers, but before his fingers could brush hers, she was jerked backward into a hard body. Two growls rose above the music. Ayana gasped. Both

Reece and Blaine had moved like lightning to make sure the man didn't come near her. She broke from Reece's hold in time to catch Blaine from jacking the dude up.

"Blaine, stop!" she yelled. If she expected everyone to get worked up and the music to stop, she was so wrong. They all kept having a good time while they watched. This madness must be normal. Ayana shook her head and tugged on Blaine's arm. "It's not a big deal. He was just asking for a dance."

Blaine didn't comment.

She sighed. "Not tonight, okay? Thanks anyway," she told the guy. He backed off, and she dragged Blaine into a hug. She rested her hands on his hips trying to force him to move. That was like making a boulder dance—it wasn't happening.

After some time, he relaxed. He drew her tight to his chest and kissed her. She nuzzled close.

"I know you're mad at me," she began, "and I know you want me to say something, but I can't yet. I…just can't."

His expression remained closed. Reece drew up behind them, and she was sandwiched between them. An embarrassed scan of the group brought relief. No one was paying them any mind. Probably because there hadn't been a fight. As she continued to look around, her gaze met Gwen's. The clear animosity was there, but Ayana was too tired to care. She rested on Blaine's chest and closed her eyes. Tomorrow was soon enough to figure everything out.

* * * *

Ayana woke up in the morning between her lovers. They'd shared a huge bed like someone knew they'd need one of its size for three people. Either that or Reece's family got freaky on a regular basis. She was exhausted beyond belief, having not slept well. That was always the case when she stayed anywhere but at home. She guessed she was a homebody, which was another strike against this relationship.

Ayana left Blaine and Reece still sleeping and showered. By the time she stepped outside the cabin, the sky was just growing light. At the edge of the clearing, Gwen came from the trees. She wore another scrap of clothing that didn't hide how beautiful she was. Ayana's insides turned. She started to head back inside, but the woman caught sight of her.

"You're not gone yet?" she sassed.

"Nope, I decided to delay it just to piss you off," Ayana snapped back.

Gwen growled. Her eyes shifted, and Ayana did everything she could to hide how it freaked her out. She remembered all too well how massive Reece had been in her living room. Gwen's smirk told her she knew Ayana was close to wetting her pants.

"Don't think Blaine is going to sniff around you long?" she said. "He was mine before, and he will be again. Remember, we're the same, but you…you're just a lowly human."

"And you're a dirty animal," Ayana countered. "Look, I'm not holding Blaine to anything. He can do what he wants. But he wants me, and if that puts your nose out of joint, all the better."

Gwen looked like she was ready to take the argument to the next level, but the door behind Ayana opened, and Reece stepped out. He drew her into his arms, casting Gwen a warning look. She sucked her teeth and flounced away.

Ayana turned in Reece's arms. "Oh Lord, if you didn't come when you did. I'm not sure I can handle all this. I mean a regular relationship is fine, but this? I don't know."

"I thought we'd settled things yesterday," he said, staring down at her.

She smiled. "You mean in the woods? Yeah, women don't settle things like that."

He grinned. "I felt very settled. But now that you mention it, I'm getting worked up again." The hardness on her belly attested to the truth of his words. She shook her head, and he grew serious. "Things will be better once we're back home."

"You might be right, but I'm beginning to think that's not reality. Not yours and Blaine's anyway."

They were on the road in an hour. Ayana elected to take the back seat of Reece's SUV so she could stretch out and try to get some sleep. She must have dozed off because the next thing she was aware of was being carried toward her house. She wiggled to get free of Blaine's arms in case someone saw them. He set her on her feet in time to catch sight of a moving truck in Brooke's driveway. Her things were being carried out one by one. In the other direction, on the same side as Brooke, another truck occupied the driveway of a different house. These people were moving in.

Ayana held her sandals in her hand and strolled barefoot to the end of the drive. The two women she'd met on her first day were strolling by.

"Hey, Ayana," they called.

She put up a hand. "Janice. Rose."

"Looks like we got another one," Janice commented.

Ayana wrinkled her nose, and the woman was all too eager to explain. "A hottie, of course. Well, he's no Blaine or Reece, but he's something to look at. Yummy!"

Of course they would have the scoop. She was surprised they weren't over there right now making a play for the new neighbor. Janice was quick to explain.

"After our walk, I'll clean up and go over to say hi. I hope there's no wife or girlfriend." She looked pointedly at Ayana. "This time, there shouldn't be any problem. I mean you can only handle so many, right?"

Oh hell no! Did she just accuse me of—

"Ladies," Reece greeted with clear dismissal in his tone and a bit of something extra. He wrapped his arms around Ayana, letting the entire neighborhood know, if not directly, surely through big mouths Janice and Rose, that they had something going on. *Like they didn't know already.*

The two women scurried along obviously afraid. Ayana glared at Reece. "Why did you do that?"

"Because they have no idea when to keep their mouths shut."

She felt his anger. Reece and Blaine were protective of her, but was it enough? Could she ignore everything she believed in coming up about choosing that special man and letting him be the one? About society's unspoken rules and what a woman should and shouldn't do?

"Come inside," he instructed.

"Reece."

"Come." He tugged her along gently leading her toward her house. "You're tired. You hardly slept last night."

"How do you know that?"

Once he got her inside the door, he whipped her up into his arms and carried her upstairs to her room. When he laid her on her bed, he leaned down over her. "We're both very aware of you at all times. You know how we feel, and we'll wait patiently for you to decide how you feel—even if it kills us."

She stroked his face. "I'm sorry."

"Don't be." He kissed her. "You have a right to decide for yourself."

"You're so understanding, Reece." She almost said she loved him. "Thanks."

Blaine came in behind him. She expected him to ignore her, but he too leaned down, taking Reece's place, and he kissed her lips. Shivering delight rocked her body. If she wasn't so exhausted, she'd ask them both to stay. But there wasn't a doubt in her mind that they'd never let her rest.

"I'll talk to you two later, okay?" she told them.

Blaine's thumb caressed her belly as he held onto her side with one big hand. She knew he didn't want to let go or leave. Reece thumped him on the back. "Come on, bear. Let's give her some time."

Now she knew the significance of that nickname and why Blaine had been annoyed every time Reece used it. She watched her bear rise and walk toward the door. She missed them both and wondered how she'd handle her feelings if she decided to break it off. At last, she was alone in her bedroom. She lay still with her eyes closed, waiting for sleep to take her. Peace was a long time in coming, but when it did, she prayed it would bring a final decision one way or another.

CHAPTER TWELVE

Ayana wandered through the pasta aisle at Bloom grocery store wondering if she wanted to make spaghetti for dinner. The way her mother and older sisters made it when she was a kid coming up meant lots of cheese and ketchup among other ingredients. She'd scarcely had an appetite over the last couple of days, and since she hadn't called for Blaine and Reece, a big pot of food was unnecessary.

She picked up her favorite pasta brand and played with the box. She couldn't decide. What was the point anyway? She missed them so much, she couldn't think straight. A decision this simple didn't take a lot of brain power, but she had just enough to keep herself pushing the cart.

"Ayana," someone called from behind her.

She turned, recognizing Janice but surprised Rose wasn't glued to her side. Ayana grunted inwardly. She was so not in the mood, but rather than just wave and move on, Janice was coming toward her. That could mean one thing only. She wanted to gossip.

"Hey, Janice," she muttered without enthusiasm. Maybe the woman would get the hint.

She didn't. "How's it going?" Janice leaned her weight all into one leg and propped an elbow on her cart handle. "Did you hear?"

Okay, so you don't give a crap how I'm doing? "What news?"

"We got Brooke back," she announced.

Ayana's eyes widened. "Brooke moved back? What is she playing musical houses? Good Lord, hasn't it only been a few days, a week at the most that she moved out?"

Janice laughed, obviously happy she'd gotten a rise out of Ayana. "Well, not Brooke exactly. But Brooke-*like*. Remember the sexy man that moved in on the corner. Well, he moved in with his sister of all people." She nodded as if Ayana had asked a question. "He's single. Anyway, his sister is almost as pretty as he is, I have to admit, and she's already making the rounds. She's got half the women hating her guts because she wears these outfits that leave nothing to the imagination. And the men are all chasing behind her. Brooke was a slut, but she didn't look like much, so you didn't have to be too nervous about your man, you know?"

"I guess," Ayana said, still not too interested and trying to think of an excuse to get away.

"But that's not all." Janice's tone of voice changed, alerting Ayana that she was about to bring up something that did interest her. The eagerness in her eyes made Ayana want to smack her and tell her to shut the hell up. Janice plowed on. "Even though it hasn't been long, everyone knows things have cooled between you and your two love toys."

Ayana gritted her teeth and flared her nostrils. "My love life has nothing to do with anyone but me."

"Tell that to Abby." Janice paused for effect. "As I drove by on the way here, I saw her talking to Blaine and Reece in front of Reece's house. They looked like they hung on her every word. Or I guess it could have been they were busy staring at her double-Ds. Who knows? Well, gotta go. See ya later."

Ayana stood where she was a good ten minutes trying to get her emotions under control. One, if Blaine and Reece were going to cheat with the new neighbor, her rushing over to their house demanding what they thought they were doing wasn't going to keep that from happening. Two, she'd brushed them off and didn't give them any indication she would accept their relationship any time soon. Technically, they hadn't broken up either, but she should trust them.

She sighed. Miserable and having come to no conclusion whatsoever, she dumped the spaghetti ingredients in her cart along with a few other items and headed to checkout. She purposely chose the longest line and walked slowly across the parking lot to her car. When her things were packed, she guided her cart back to the front of the store rather than use a convenient storage place on the lot. At this point, she didn't know if she delayed going back so she wouldn't catch sight of them talking and zap out, or if she hoped they'd be dumb enough to reveal themselves as cheaters and invite the woman into the house.

She was pathetic, and her heart ached to be with them. After sliding behind the wheel of her car and turning over the engine, she reached a hand to her cheek. Tears had wet them.

A few minutes later, she pulled into her driveway. They were still out there. She gritted her teeth. Janice's description of the woman had been an understatement. She was gorgeous with a voluptuous figure and long flaming blonde hair. On a cool breeze, her laughter reached Ayana.

She slipped out of her car with her eyes lowered in annoyance and moved toward the trunk. To her surprise, she bumped into Reece's broad chest. When the hell had he left Ms. Thing's side? The stir of her bags beside her caught her attention. Blaine was already pulling the groceries out. Ayana glanced over toward Blaine's lawn. The woman stood there, mouth hanging open, brows in her hairline. She couldn't believe the men had left her so fast to run over to Ayana.

Ayana's lips twitched as she tried to keep herself from smiling. "You two seemed happy where you were just now."

Reece nabbed her door keys from her hand. "Baby, you should have told us you were going to the grocery store. We could have helped you with the bags. Did someone assist you with getting them in the trunk?"

"I'm not so frail." She waited for them to say something about the half-naked tramp in front of Blaine's house, but then she began to see as they unpacked the food that the woman wasn't a blip in their existence. She wondered if they'd been out there so long only so they wouldn't miss her return. "Um, you really didn't think twice about that woman, did you?"

Blaine looked up from contemplating the ground turkey she'd bought. Crap she knew she should have gone with beef.

"Why would we?" he asked.

Reece took the package of cheese she held and set it on the table. He tugged out a chair and drew her onto his lap when he sat down. "You are our mate. I don't know how many ways we can say it or how we can convince you. Ayana, there is no other woman for us. Ever."

She blinked. "Ever? You mean like no divorce or change of mind or growing out of love?"

"Pretty much."

Ayana stared from one handsome face to the other. She wrapped her arms around Reece's neck and rested her head on his shoulder. "This scares me. I can't get over the fear."

"And you won't. Not yet," he assured her. "All relationships are that way at first. It's exciting but scary. I can tell you that our kind mates for life, but with the society we live in, it's incomprehensible to you. You feel like no one could know that up front, that it'll last."

"Yeah. You hit it on the head."

"Okay, think about it a different way."

She watched the confidence leave his expression and something deeper, more emotional take its place. He studied her face, stroked her skin, and even seemed to breathe in her scent as if he wanted to write it on his memory. Blaine's expression wasn't so open, but once again, she saw the anger and couldn't understand why he was so upset.

"You are human," Reece announced.

"Uh, yeah, I knew that."

He smiled at her. She could lose herself in his smile the rest of her life.

"You are not like us," he said simply. She was almost offended until she realized what he was saying. "At any time, your feelings could change. You could decide you're tired of us and want something different. You could meet some other man and want to be with him. Our very makeup directs us toward bonding with our mate. It's a lock that can't be undone except in death. You are not bound in such a way."

Ayana pressed her hand to her mouth, eyes wide as the full impact of what he was saying got through. She looked at Blaine and knew now why he was angry. Not because he was mad but because he was vulnerable—to her and her human whims.

Blaine didn't like having his control wrenched from his hands, but that's basically what happened. Her two lovers had waited around for her not because they decided to, but because they had to. They had no more existence without her. Their full happiness was wrapped up in whether Ayana accepted what she felt for them and what they felt for her.

She cried a little more than she had earlier in the grocery store parking lot. "Your risk is way more than mine, isn't it?" They didn't say anything, but she knew the answer was yes. The weight of it was a lot to put on her, and deep inside she wanted to high tail it out of there. But she'd been miserable without them.

Ayana hugged Reece and reached her hand out to Blaine. He took it and held it in his huge palm. "As unusual as our relationship is, it's like any other—scary and exciting, and uncertain in a way. I know what I feel now." She smiled at Blaine, and the anger disappeared from his eyes. "I love you. And I love you too, Reece. I want us to be together no matter what anyone says or thinks."

Reece crushed her in his arms until she yelped, and he loosened his hold. Blaine scooted his chair closer. He reached out and drew her onto his lap facing him. His rough kisses and hands running along her sides got her worked up. He buried his face in her hair. "I love you, Ayana. I'll protect you and take care of you."

"I know." She nuzzled closer to him while watching Reece over her shoulder. His hand rested on her back, a thumb massaging her skin through her blouse. "What I don't know is how we'll pull it off, but damn it, I'm willing. I'm not letting either of you go anymore. That means no skank gets to come on your lawn and shake her wares in your faces."

Reece threw his head back laughing. "Yes, ma'am. Whatever you say."

She glared at Blaine too. "Got that, bear?"

He grinned. "Loud and clear. We're all yours. Forever."

Satisfied, Ayana leaned back from Blaine and lifted her blouse over her head. Her small breasts strained at her bra, they were so achy for her lovers' touches. At the moment, she had not one shred of jealousy for the woman outside. The two sexy shifters had chosen her, and there were no trade backs.

She stood up and stripped off the rest of her clothes as she walked toward the kitchen door. At the entry, she paused and glanced back at the shocked men whose eyes were riveted to her naked figure. "So who wants to seal it with a kiss?"

They scrambled after her, and with a full heart, Ayana jetted for the stairs, content with who she was and what she wanted at last.

The End

Bear NECESSITIES

CHAPTER ONE

Simone threw her bag out the car door and gave the driver her brightest smile. "Thanks, Boo. You're sweet for bringing me so far out of your way." She eased out of the low-rider car knowing he wasn't focused on her lips but on her ass, what with the booty shorts she was wearing. Let him look. He sure wasn't going to get a feel. She knew how to work her figure and wrap men around her little finger. Hell, she'd been playing the game long enough.

"You sure you don't need me to take you to your sister's door?" he called over the music blaring from the speakers. "It's getting kind of late, and I don't want anything to happen to you."

When she turned around and leaned on the door, his gaze shifted to her cleavage. "No, I'm good. Thanks. Besides, with that tent in your pants, I might need to watch myself with you more than anyone else out here. Later."

He chuckled at her boldness, and she waved a hand as she hoisted her bag onto her shoulder. While she walked down the side of the road, she fished her cell phone out of her pocket and began scrolling through her contact list. Now that she was in Charlotte, there was no way her cousin Ayana would turn her away.

Before she left New York, her friends had said North Carolina was all country. Their ignorant asses had told her there were no malls, and there was no way she should go down to a backwater place like Charlotte. The nearest store was miles away, she'd been told, but as she walked along, she found that it was no different from any other city she'd seen. Except that it was nicer, she thought. So far, she'd come across gas stations, convenience stores, and even Walmart. As far as she was concerned if they had that, she was good.

The call went through to her cousin right away, and she waited with knotted stomach for an answer. After a few rings, Ayana picked up. "Hello?"

"Hey, cuz," Simone chirped into the phone. "It's me. I'm here in Charlotte. Just thought I'd drop by."

"What?" Ayana almost shouted. "Are you serious, Simone? Dropping by isn't like I live down the street."

"I know. And what?" Simone said. "I needed a change, so I'm here. Girl, you gonna give me a ride to your place or what?"

She could almost hear Ayana gritting her teeth. A man's voice sounded in the background, and Simone grinned shaking her head. So her cousin was getting some action down here. She didn't blame her but hoped she wasn't interrupting too much.

"Where are you?" Ayana said at last.

Only then did Simone realize she wasn't exactly sure. "Oh wow, um, let me check at a gas station or something and call you back."

Ayana sighed. "Fine." She hung up.

Half an hour later, Simone was riding in an SUV sitting behind the most gorgeous man she'd ever seen. She leaned forward in her back seat and held out her hand. "How are you? I'm Simone, Ayana's cousin."

The amusement in his eyes made her tingle with awareness. "Reece," he said in a deep voice.

"Yum," she cooed, but Ayana glared at her. Simone settled back and waited until they turned off a busy road onto a side one. She squinted to catch sight of the street sign and read Lawnwood Drive. The houses were all residential single-family homes. This was a nice difference from where she was from. She and her mother had lived in an apartment in the ghetto, and it was all they could do to keep their heads above water.

Of course her mother had taken it upon herself to better their circumstances by latching onto any available man with a job. Never mind whether he was a good person or not. Through all that Simone had learned how to take care of herself when it came to men. And only when her mother thought she was in love with the latest loser too free with his hands and Simone's ass did she feel their living together didn't work. Simone had left the same day. She was twenty-eight, and she could damn sure handle her own business without her mother.

"I thought we talked about you visiting sometime, but we hadn't settled on when," Ayana commented as they pulled up into the driveway at her house.

"Things got a little hot, so I had to get out of there," Simone commented, but her attention was on the second hottie just stepping out of Ayana's house. She froze when the man strolled down the drive and took Ayana into his arms. They murmured something to each other, and he kissed her on the lips before running his big hands down to her ass for a squeeze.

Simone's mouth dropped open. She swung her gaze from the man holding her cousin to Reece. He walked over to the other man with his hand stuck out, and they shook on friendly terms. "I thought you wouldn't be back until tomorrow night."

The darker man nodded. "I wanted to get back to Ayana. I don't like being away too long even if she has you to protect her."

Reece seemed to understand completely. The three of them were so wrapped up in each other that they didn't pay Simone any mind. She put her hands on her hips and frowned. "Ayana, just what the hell you got going on down here, girl?"

Her cousin started a little and turned wary eyes on Simone. A noise from across the street kept her from saying a word. Someone slammed a door, and a woman obviously in tears yelled, "I can handle things on my own!"

All four of them swung around to face the house on the opposite corner. Simone watched a woman with flaming red hair that could only have been created in a bottle come storming down her driveway. She wrenched open the door on a minivan and began unloading it. The bland dress she wore stood out in the descending dusk only because it was so plain and did nothing for her plus-size figure. She wasn't bad-looking, but *damn woman, flaunt what you got a little.*

Simone spun to face her cousin. "New neighbors?"

The words and teasing attitude died on her lips when she spotted yet a third man coming from Ayana's house. This one didn't immediately go over to Ayana to kiss and touch her like a lover, but Simone couldn't help noticing that he was just big as the other two. He had a feral quality about him, and his dark hair hung too long as a few strands swept across his rugged features. She couldn't say he was handsome exactly, but he had his appeal. The eyes were a color she couldn't define in the growing darkness, but she sensed the danger in their depths, and it sent chills racing up and down her spine. His lips were chiseled to thick yet soft-looking perfection. His body was hard and muscled. He wore cargo pants and nothing else, leaving his chest bare so she could feast her eyes on its smooth tanned expanse.

"Who's this?" Ayana asked, and Simone couldn't believe the relief she felt knowing this man wasn't in her cousin's male harem.

Sexy walked up to her cousin with a friendly grin on his face. She guessed he was in his early thirties. "I'm Artan. You must be his mate Ayana. Good to meet you."

Artan. That was different. Simone sidled up to him and smiled. Wow, she had to tip her head way back to look into his face. "I'm Simone."

When his eyes lit on her they widened, and his brows nearly disappeared into his hairline. "You," he breathed. The one word was so sensual, it felt like a caress. He took Simone's hand and brought it to his lips but not to kiss as she thought. He seemed to take her in with a single breath. A sudden impulse to squeeze her legs together took hold of her, but she resisted it. "You're why he wouldn't… He smelled you miles before you got here."

Simone blinked at him. Damn. Sexy was crazy. "Come again?"

"Let's go inside," Ayana interrupted. "We don't need to put on more of a show for the neighborhood than we already have." She herded everyone inside, and Simone was happy with the fact that Artan hadn't let her hand go. He walked at her side and stepped back a little to allow her to pass ahead of him into the house. Manners. She liked that.

Ayana went around clicking on lights in her living room and directing them to take seats. Despite how much she wanted to know about the man who hadn't let her go yet, she was also curious about why her cousin was keeping house with two men and they were okay with it. Last time she checked, Ayana was not that good with men.

When she settled on the couch, she smiled to find that Artan was happy to drop at her feet and rest his head in her lap. He was sweet, so she didn't push him away for his presumptuousness. Instead, she started playing in his silky hair and wondered how he'd look with a braid on each side.

"So, cousin," she said, looking up at Ayana, "what's up with you keeping two men?"

"Before that," Reece interrupted, "Blaine, you want to explain why you brought a strange man into our home?"

Blaine, so that was her other lover's name, Simone thought. He hadn't left Ayana's side either, and while he hid his emotions from showing on his face, she got the impression he loved her cousin. A spark of jealousy rose inside of her, but she tamped it down. Simone didn't believe in love like the storybooks, so it was no sense getting worked up.

"Remember how I thought I had no family?" Blaine explained. "Well my visit to South Carolina this time proved me wrong. Artan has been looking for more of his people, and he showed me proof that indicated we're cousins several times removed."

"Family," both Ayana and Simone echoed at the same time. Simone frowned thinking Ayana meant her with the negative tone to her voice. Simone referred to her mother.

"Well we can talk about it at the dinner table," Ayana said. "I'm starving." She swirled around to face Simone. "For the record, yes, I have two lovers—Blaine and Reece. You have a problem with it, you can go back home."

Simone laughed at the defensiveness in her cousin's words and held up her hands. "Please, more power to you, girl. I never thought you had it in you. I wish I had two yummies like them."

Artan raised his head, a frown of confusion on his face. "But of course you do. Me and my brother."

She blinked at him, but then, as if he'd spoken, everyone turned to look to the man suddenly standing in the kitchen doorway with an angry glare on his face. This fourth man was the spitting image of Artan and was even more sparsely dressed.

CHAPTER TWO

The silence in the room was broken by Simone's muttered, "Damn." The man looked like Tarzan. He wasn't exactly wearing a loincloth or anything, but he might as well be. The shorts didn't completely cover his tan, muscled legs, and the way they outlined his crotch had her ready to pant. Or maybe he had a lot of junk inside them. She didn't know. A longing to find out took hold of her, and she bit her fingernail. Someone cleared their throat, and Simone forced her gaze up from the man's goods.

"Who's this?" she asked. She really hoped her cousin didn't miscalculate the number of men she had in her bed.

Artan popped up from the floor and pulled Simone to her feet. With firm hands at her waist, he shuffled her over to the man in the doorway. "Brother, this is our mate. I'm sure you can tell that already. Isn't she beautiful?" He dipped his head toward her neck as if to smell her. "And her scent..."

Simone swatted him away. "I think I missed something here. What's with all the 'mate' stuff?"

"Artan," Blaine barked. "Are you sure about that?"

The man who hadn't spoken was the one who answered instead of Artan. He sighed as if long-suffering fools. "He is sure. However"—his hot gaze turned from Blaine to Simone, and she shifted from one foot to the other—"I do not accept her."

"Oh, hold up. No you didn't," she shrieked. "You do not accept me? For the record, I'm not for sale or whatever y'all are talking about. Ayana, you want to explain to me what this is about?"

Ayana walked toward the kitchen, and Mr. Full-of-Himself stepped aside to let her pass. "We'll talk over dinner," she said.

Artan, in his happy eagerness, propelled her forward, and they all piled into the little kitchen. Simone would have thought the place was more spacious than the tiny apartment she and her mother had shared most of her life, but with four big men crowding it, she felt suffocated.

Ayana was efficient in getting them all settled and sitting around the table as she set out plates and big dishes of food. She might not have known Blaine and the twins were coming, but she sure had prepared for them. Simone wondered what her weekly grocery bill was like.

The twins were the only two who seemed a bit uncomfortable at the table, Artan less than the other guy. Simone had been sandwiched between the two of them, which wouldn't have been a bad thing except it was painfully clear that Artan's brother hated her guts for no reason at all. Well he wasn't all that either, she decided.

She couldn't help but lean over to Artan and whisper, "What's the stuffed shirt's name?" Artan chuckled, and his brother grunted. Guess they had good hearing.

"Fallyn," Artan supplied. "Don't mind him. He's never been to the city before. Well, neither have I, but I'm liking it a lot. Fallyn doesn't do well around people for long. He tolerates infrequent visits to the gatherings on our lands. There we have those who spend all their time in civilization, those who split it fifty-fifty, and a few like Fallyn and I who have fully embraced our animal side and are content with nature."

Simone was nodding like she knew what the hell he was talking about, but by the time Artan finished explaining his brother's attitude problem, she was more lost. Since she'd traveled a long way to get here, Simone decided to focus on her food, which consisted of baked tilapia, potatoes, corn on the cob, green beans, and homemade biscuits. The food was delicious, but then most of the women in her family were good cooks. Her grandmother had attributed it to her great-grandmother who was born and raised in Carthage, North Carolina. She supposed she should view coming to Charlotte as a sort of coming home.

"This is really good, Ayana," she commented, hoping to soothe her cousin's ruffled feathers for her showing up uninvited. "You always cook for an army?"

Ayana's nostrils flared, and she squinted her eyes at Simone. Guess she'd said the wrong thing again. "The guys have big appetites, so I'm used to cooking a lot even though I didn't expect Blaine back so soon. It's a good thing since Artan and Fallyn are here too."

"So," Simone continued in as casual a tone as she could muster, "what's with the 'animal side' thing and the whole 'gatherings on our lands'?"

Every hand froze on the way to their lips. No one said a word. Simone had never minded much having all eyes on her, but this was ridiculous. She wiggled in her seat and glanced around. Artan was pretty open from what she'd seen so far, but even he didn't answer her question. To her surprise, the one who spoke up was Fallyn.

At the first rumble of his deep voice, she'd twisted around to face him and watched how prickly he appeared. No matter what Artan had said, she didn't think it was being around people that had him annoyed so much. The way he eyed her like she was some kind of bug was a blow to her self-esteem.

"We are shifters," he announced. "To be specific bear shifters."

She stared. "Shifters?" She didn't want to say more than what he had in case she looked like a complete fool for not understanding. He caught on that she didn't get it anyway and frowned.

"Shape-shifters. We can turn into bears," he elaborated.

"You lying." She laughed and looked around to her cousin. "He looks like he believes that nonsense. Dude, this is not the sci-fi channel, but I'll give you props for interesting dinner conversation."

She reached out to pat his arm knowing she patronized him, but he snarled in anger. In a flash of movement, Artan jerked her chair back and was standing between her and Fallyn. They were chest to chest, teeth bared, glaring at each other. Artan's easygoing attitude was gone in an instant.

"Calm down, brother," he snapped. "You make a mistake and hurt her in your anger, we're going to have a problem."

Fallyn sneered. "Don't be stupid."

Simone stood up realizing that everyone else was on their feet too. Her throat was dry, and her limbs felt shaky. Had Fallyn intended to hit her or something? She didn't think so, but Artan should know him better. A simple conversation had gone wrong in like seconds. She couldn't believe what was going on now, let alone what Fallyn had said. Every person at the table from their expressions had taken his claim very seriously, and there wasn't one look of surprise like what was washing through her right then.

"Artan," Reece said. Simone wondered why he didn't get on Fallyn instead. "He would never do that. If like you think, she…uh…you've found your mate, then it's not possible for Fallyn to hurt her."

Reece was trying to avoid saying they thought she was their mate. She was no idiot. She got the meaning, and if they did think they were some kind of animal or whatever, then *mate* would be the word they'd use. Either way, they were wrong. Simone squeezed by the small crowd in the kitchen and headed for the door. She ignored Ayana calling out to her as she went out outside.

In the driveway, she leaned against Reece's SUV and closed her eyes. The sun had gone down, and a breeze stirred her hair about her face. The air here was sweeter and cleaner than where she had lived with her mother. She'd thought coming here would be perfect, but it was starting out freaking nutty. Every person in that house must have lost their minds, including Ayana if they wanted her to believe they were some kind of shifters. She considered it and then wondered if it was like the Native Americans who believed in spirit guides. Thinking about it that way eased her mind a little.

When the door opened again, she glanced around to find Ayana standing there. She sighed. “You going to ask me to go back to New York?”

Ayana took up a spot beside her and stared down at the ground with her hands tucked under her butt to protect from the chill of the vehicle. “No, I’m not. We’re past that.”

“What do you mean?”

She hesitated and then looked at Simone. “Listen, sweetie, I know you think we’re crazy, and if it was left up to me, I wouldn’t have told you anything. Definitely not on your first night, but they do things differently. I’m just meeting Artan and Fallyn too, and so is Blaine. All I know for sure is they—well Artan—has his eye on you. If you like him and want to see where it goes, fine. If not, I’ll get Blaine to make him back off. At this point, I don’t think you have anything to worry about when it comes to Fallyn.”

“Because he can’t stand me,” Simone agreed.

“I don’t think it’s that.”

She rolled her eyes. “Whatever. He doesn’t know me like that anyway. So what have you been doing down here in the boonies other than banging two sexy men?”

Ayana laughed. “Hardly the boonies.”

They both looked toward the street when a man drove up on the opposite side in front of the end house. He stepped out and drew on a cigarette before tossing it away. Simone pursed her lips. She hated people who littered, especially with cigarettes. She’d had a friend coming up who used to chain smoke on her balcony and thought she could throw the butts down and not clean them up. Simone disabused girlfriend of that crap real quick.

The man straightened his clothes and happened to look over in their direction. His interest perked up, and he looked like he was about to approach them, but Ayana's door was flung open and all four men barreled outside headed in his direction. Simone gasped.

"Damn, did you see that? They have bloodhound nostrils or what?" She shook her head laughing. "Then again, men always did sense when another one was even thinking about horning in on their territory. Your guys watch you like a hawk?"

Ayana smirked. "Notice there's two more than I claim out here."

Simone followed her line of vision. Even Fallyn had come although she didn't know why. Hell, if he didn't want her, why should she limit herself? The smoker held up his hands and backed up. He spun on his heels and headed up to the house across the street. That had been the same one where she'd seem the woman arguing with an older couple. Guess she had company tonight too. Just what kind of neighborhood did Ayana live in?

"Reece, Blaine, it's fine," Ayana called. "He wasn't interested in us. Leave the poor man alone."

By the time they go back to the house, her food was cold. Simone helped Ayana clean up the kitchen and wash the dishes. When she was done, she took her bag up to the spare bedroom Ayana directed her to, and she took a shower to wash away the grime of the road. If all the craziness of the night hadn't happened, she would have done it long before now.

The men filled the space in the small living room. The night had turned cold, so Reece started a fire in the fireplace. When Simone joined them, she found Fallyn crouched near the floor examining a leather pack in his hand, and Artan parked on the floor in front of the fireplace. An oversize throw pillow lay at his side, and he patted it when she walked into the room.

"If I had any common sense," she told him, "I'd be catching the first bus or train home. The problem with that is I'm broke, and I can't face traveling another step." She dropped down on the pillow beside him, and Artan played with a lock of her hair. She brushed his hand away. Not being mean, but firm about him watching his hands. "You do not touch a black woman's hair, man."

His eyes widened. "Really?"

"Yes, really." She eyed him a few minutes. His body was big and hard, and with him still hardly dressed, she got to enjoy every ripple in his abs and the way his skin stretched taut over the plains and sinews. Artan's eyes matched those of his brother, deep blue like the ocean, and his hair was thick and black like midnight. He and Fallyn both looked like they didn't believe in haircuts, but looking at them, it wasn't a bad thing. Goodness knows even crazy, Artan was too much to resist. "So you've never been to the city?"

He shook his head. "No. Just today."

"But you've been around civilization, right? I mean it's impossible not to unless you mean y'all were raised in the country." Simone had no real idea what she was asking. Maybe she just couldn't comprehend two people so cut off. She must be jumping to conclusions. "You've seen all this."

She gestured to their surroundings and Ayana's furnishings. Artan nodded, and Simone breathed a sigh of relief.

"Oh goodness, you had me going there for a second." She laid a hand on her chest, and he followed the movement, his eyes lingering on her cleavage. Simone had decent sized breasts as far as she was concerned—not too big and not too small. She liked to wear clothes that played them up, and from the looks of it, Artan appreciated what he saw. She enjoyed having men look at her, but not other women's men, unlike what her mother accused her of.

After a few minutes, Artan lifted a hand as if he intended to grab her breast, but she slapped his hand. He rubbed it and raised his eyes to meet hers. Amusement lay in the blue depths. She couldn't be mad at him. He wasn't that innocent.

"We have houses on our lands. They have most of this. Not all. But my people who live there are simple in their needs."

She nodded. "Hm, the bare necessities. Yeah, I'm not the one. I don't travel anywhere or stay any place without my makeup, my hair products, and my clothes." She ticked them off on her fingers, and just by his cute expression, she knew dog on well Artan didn't know what she was talking about. "Do not tell me your people don't wear makeup. I'm not going to believe it."

"Face paint," Fallyn said, making her realize he'd been listening to their conversation all along. She looked over her shoulder and rolled her eyes at him. Annoyance radiated from him, and she turned away.

She faced Artan in time for him to touch fingertips to her cheek. "This stuff," he said in wonder at her foundation. She'd taken the time to refresh her makeup before coming back downstairs. With this many men, she wanted to look her best. Artan's mesmerized look seemed to make the time well worth spending. "You would look more beautiful without it."

She tried pulling away from him, but he caught her wrist and tugged her closer. She glared at him. "You didn't just insult me."

"No, you're beautiful," he said, still staring. She shifted on the pillow. "You're more beautiful underneath. I can tell. Can I kiss you?"

She couldn't help blushing, which was ridiculous because men tossed compliments her way all the time. But many of them in New York had thought they had the right to get free with their hands just because she stopped to have a conversation with them. She'd never been asked permission for a kiss. That was new—and sweet.

"You're cute." She patted his cheek. "But no." Artan must have assumed she'd say yes, because when she didn't, he sat there stunned. Simone used the opportunity to slip out of his grasp and stand up. "Well, it's late. I'm going to bed. Nice meeting all of you."

She walked toward the stairs, and Artan sprung to his feet to follow.

Simone held up a hand. "Oh no, homeboy, I just met you. I don't know where you're sleeping tonight, but it's not going to be with me."

Leaving Artan looking crushed, she headed upstairs. Halfway up and just about to pass out of view of them, she couldn't resist looking over to where Fallyn sat. He was still examining his pouch, and she wondered what was so damn interesting in it that he couldn't carry on a conversation like a normal person.

She headed up to her room and shut the door. After removing her makeup and clothes, she dug out her favorite nightie. The sky blue piece was a shimmery number that reached just below her snatch. She put it on and dropped into bed.

Somewhere around one in the morning, she woke up from a deep sleep to the sound of Ayana crying out in pleasure as apparently one, the other, or both of her lovers took her to extreme sexual heights. Simone gritted her teeth and yanked the comforter over her head. Nothing blocked out the noises coming from across the hall, and her own desires began to kick in.

In a matter of seconds her pussy was drenched, and she tossed and turned in the bed while squeezing her legs together. She didn't really want to get herself off while listening to her cousin. Somehow that seemed gross, but it didn't stop her wanting sex bad.

When she heard a gruff command and what was clearly a smack against skin, she stuffed the edge of her pillow into her mouth. *Oh goodness, now he's spanking her!* Simone squeezed her eyes shut and groaned.

A step just outside her door made her quiet down. Someone was in the hall. She frowned. One or both of those perverted twins were up there listening to Ayana. Anger and jealousy rose inside her, and she thrust the covers back to rise and tiptoe over to the door. When she wrenched it open, she found both twins in the hall. Fallyn was at the top of the stairs, but Artan had come all the way up. What made her catch her breath was that both men were facing her door and not Ayana's. In fact, Artan was so close, he could reach out and touch her.

"W-What are you doing?" she whispered.

Neither of them answered. The sex in the next room was still going on at disturbing volumes, but Artan and Fallyn were staring at her. Simone glanced down and shrieked. Above the hall was a beautiful skylight, and the moon chose that moment to shine its shimmery glow in the hall. Simone's nipples were clearly defined behind her nightie, and the only reason the men couldn't see her pussy was because the hem had a line of ruching, which was not see through.

Simone slapped her hands over her breasts and her crotch anyway and backed up. She kicked the door closed and spun around to return to bed. *Note to self: get a damn robe with all these men running around the house.*

"Simone?" Artan called.

"Go away, idiot. We're not doing what they are," she yelled.

There were male whispers in the hall, and then Ayana's group quieted. She sighed in relief and rolled over. Sleep didn't come for another couple of hours, and then she dreamed of two sexy twins giving her pleasure that could only be in a fantasy.

CHAPTER THREE

Simone's eyes hurt, and she had a headache. She'd smelled coffee for the last hour but hadn't been able to make herself get out of bed. She'd have to face them. Somehow she forced herself up and showered and brushed her teeth. When she was dressed, she moved down the stairs, doing everything she could not to jar her head. At the base of the stairs, she paused hearing Ayana discussing the twins.

"You know they were out in the hall last night, right?" Ayana said.

Blaine grunted, and Reece chuckled. "Yes, but don't worry. They weren't listening to us."

"How do you know?"

"Because Simone was listening," he answered. Hearing that she snarled, ready to go read him. She didn't need to get off listening to them have sex. And if they had any courtesy for their guests, they wouldn't have been so damn loud.

"Okay, what the heck to you mean by that?" Ayana sounded just as annoyed as she was. *Hello? Cousins. That's gross.*

"Because the sounds of sex got her excited, and because she was, Artan and Fallyn smelled it."

Simone's mouth dropped open. She stared blankly at the front door unmoving. Reece went on to explain what sounded to her like more craziness.

"You remember the bear can smell up to twenty miles away? It helps us track food and our mates. So you can imagine how strong Simone's scent was in their noses last night. They wouldn't be able to do much other than come to her. She doesn't understand what we are or what it means for them to claim her. Fallyn might resist, but I don't see him holding out for long."

"Yeah," Blaine agreed. "Otherwise, he would have already left. My guess is he can't bring himself to do it. Last night was only the beginning."

"So maybe we should go to your house or to Reece's," Ayana suggested.

Simone chose that moment to walk in on them. "Maybe you should if you're going to be so damn loud every night. I couldn't sleep!"

The amusement on Reece's face irritated her. "Glad to entertain."

She rolled her eyes. "Bite me."

"Maybe I should remind you that you're the one who invited yourself, Simone," Ayana griped. "But I do think we should make some adjustments with the arrangements. I don't want to leave you alone with Artan and Fallyn."

Simone poured herself a cup of coffee. "What am I, eight?"

"You wouldn't understand."

She ignored her cousin and looked around the kitchen. Artan and Fallyn weren't there, and she hadn't seen them passing through from the living room either. The second floor held only two bedrooms, so she knew they weren't up there. Somehow the thought of them returning to the country or wherever they came from got to her. At least Artan leaving did. "Where are the twins?"

"They weren't here when we woke up," Blaine told her.

Simone put her hand on her hip. "Let me get this straight. You let two half-naked men who've never been to the city loose in Charlotte?"

Blaine's eyebrows drew together, and his lips grew white he pressed them together so hard. He was obviously worried, and she hadn't made it any better. "I know where they are. I just stated they weren't here when I woke up. I suspect they went to a particular area we passed on the way up here. If they are not back soon, I'll go after them."

"And for the record," Ayana added, "I had Reece give them clothes. Since I don't see the things lying around, I assume the guys aren't naked." Her eyes took on an amused look. "I didn't know you cared so much having just met them."

Simone sucked her teeth. "Don't even."

She drained her cup of coffee and poured more. After she'd stirred in some sugar, she wandered over to the front door and opened it. The street was quiet. Two rows of houses with big front lawns ran down its length. The residences weren't cookie-cutter in the least with some brick and some with siding in an assortment of colors, but it still had that cutesy feel to the block that Simone wasn't used to seeing. The jury was still out on whether or not she liked it.

While she stood watching, a young girl about six came riding along on her bike. She hit a bump in the sidewalk, and went down hard. Simone sucked in a breath and took a step forward, but then she stopped when she saw Fallyn bend down to help the girl. He hadn't been there a minute ago, but then he could have been behind Reece's SUV. She watched to see what he would do and was surprised by the gentle expression on his face and the way he helped the girl up.

She'd skinned her knee and stood there whining. Simone couldn't hear what Fallyn was saying, but the girl nodded at whatever it was. Fallyn pulled out his leather pouch and loosened the strings around it. She squinted to see what he pulled out and decided it was some kind of leaf. "Oh goodness, Blaine, you better get your boy," she called over her shoulder. "He's giving a little girl some kind of herb."

Blaine brushed by her in a heartbeat, but Simone hadn't taken her eyes off Fallyn. He crouched on one knee and was holding the little girl's leg while rubbing the herb on her scratch. On the breeze, Simone caught her giggle. "It tickles."

Before long, the girl was on her merry way riding more carefully, and Simone listened while Blaine lectured Fallyn about messing with other people's kids. He might have been wrong, but she'd seen the tenderness and caring in his actions.

Fallyn listened in rapt attention to what Blaine had to say, and then gave a curt nod. When he turned toward her, his expression grew darker. She sighed guessing he was pissed she hadn't warned him directly. Simone walked right by him and caught his brother's arm as he came up. "Walk with me?" She batted her eyes at him.

Artan grinned. "Of course."

They circled the block a couple times and ventured farther. Simone chatted about her life in New York, careful not to mention the parts that she didn't want anyone to know. She told him about partying and dating and the sites to see. Artan listened to her as if his life depended on her words, and she liked it.

"So what about you?" she asked him when she'd exhausted her topics. "What did you spend your life doing out in the woods?"

Artan shrugged. "Hunting, taking care of the family, mating…"

"Mating! I thought—" She bit the inside of her cheek. "Uh, so what did you do for money? Don't you have a job?"

The amusement in his eyes made her grind her teeth. He leaned in close to her ear and let his warm lips brush her lobe. A shiver raced down her spine. "Mating in this case means sex. We have high sex drives. I could have shown you my skill if you had let me in your room last night."

His words had her panties wet, and the way he flared his nostrils and took in a deep breath, she had a feeling he could smell it. Who the hell were these men? She cleared her throat. "Anyway…"

He let the matter drop since she wasn't even going there. "We have investments mostly. Our finances are shared throughout the family. No one is left with a need unmet. Since I don't have much need for anything and I get what I do from the land, I don't have much use for money."

Simone frowned. “In other words, you’re broke.”

He looked down at himself. That’s when she noticed his earlier words had caused his cock to get hard. From the looks of the bulge in the jeans he’d been given to put on, he was so not damaged. *Good golly, Ms. Molly.* She blew out a heavy breath.

“I meant you don’t have any money. I don’t usually go out with guys that don’t have any,” she told him.

“Is it important to you?”

“Kind of. Yeah.” She looked ahead of them and realized she had no idea how they got to the street they were on or how to get back to Ayana’s place. “Don’t get me wrong. I take care of myself, but the jobs I’ve held down aren’t all that. They paid the bills I was responsible for and nothing more.”

He stopped walking and turned to face her. When he took hold of her chin and raised it so that she had to look in his eyes, Simone shivered. The man was too sexy for his own good. Sure, she’d dated gorgeous men, and if she got involved with Artan, he wouldn’t be the first white man she’d sampled. But there was so much to him, something she couldn’t put her finger on. Whatever that magnetism was, it didn’t let her dwell too much on the fact that he was a little too into the whole spirit guide thing.

“We can take care of you,” he said. “My brother and I.”

“He doesn’t want me.” She didn’t know the man, yet it kind of smarted that he didn’t. Fallyn’s attitude put her in mind of the past when she’d gone running behind that no good ass of a father of hers. Back then she didn’t know how to manipulate men to get what she wanted. She’d had her heart wide open, and he’d stomped on it.

“Don’t call me daddy,” he’d insisted. *“I don’t know if you’re mine. That’s what your mother said, but I don’t have any kids.”*

She’d been crushed, and she’d stood there in silence while her mother cussed him out. Simone guessed in some ways she and her mother were doing the same thing since then, either punishing men or making them plead for a taste. The whole thing was too damn textbook, so she didn't think of it often. Of course, Fallyn and Artan were bringing it all back in the half day of knowing them.

She pulled out of his hold. "Thanks, sweetie, but we already established you don't have more than the cargo pants you were wearing last night." She smiled. "I'll enjoy the view for a little while."

He didn't seem to get that she meant his scrumptious body, but he didn't press. Artan was easygoing and seemed to take everything in stride. Simone walked ahead of him, arms slightly raised so she could enjoy the warm summer day. Spring and summer were her favorites, and she hibernated in winter. Coming out in the cold in New York just wasn't worth it, but Ayana had told her the last time she spoke with her before she came that in North Carolina the chilly seasons were milder. That was something to look forward to.

At the corner, Simone stopped walking and looked back. "Tell me you know where the heck we are because I am so lost."

Artan strolled with his hands in his jean pockets. His fists caused his pants to strain over his package. Simone sighed. She had a rule. No sex on the first date. The second or third either, but then they hadn't had their first. That was another thing she hadn't decided on. She should really focus on getting settled, but she was never without a man long. Love was a whole other issue. She didn't need it because it made a woman weak.

"I know the way," he told her, and she fell into step beside him.

"Are you smelling it?" she asked. Maybe all that country living opened up the senses more.

"Yes."

She chewed her bottom lip for a minute. "Do you really think you can turn into a bear?"

"No."

She sighed in relief.

"I *know* it."

Simone groaned. And then since she never allowed herself to stay down long, she asked, "How about you help me discover the hot spots in this town? You staying long?"

He nodded. "I will be here as long as you are." When she noticed he wasn't focused on her but on something ahead, she turned to look. Somehow they'd found their way back to Lawnwood Drive, and the woman in the tent dress was talking to Fallyn. Even from their distance, Simone could see that she was flirting. She threw back her head and laughed at something Fallyn said and then laid a hand on his forearm. She moved closer to him and then had the nerve to brush her breast against his arm.

"No that bitch didn't," Simone muttered. But then she dismissed it. Fallyn wasn't hers, and she didn't want him. Artan was more interesting, and she had the feeling he'd do whatever she suggested. She focused on him instead of his brother as they continued toward the house. "So, you're game to go wherever I want?"

"Of course," he assured her. "I can only convince you that we belong together if we spend time in each other's company. And of course, I must protect you."

She smiled. "From other wild animals?"

"There are none around here to hurt you."

She started to ask how he knew but didn't bother. Against her will, her attention returned to Fallyn and the slut. She thought of the little girl he'd wrapped around his finger and now Ms. Thing. "He has his own way of charming women, I guess."

"Are you interested?" Artan asked.

She sucked her teeth. "Are you jealous?"

"Why would I be? He's my brother, and we've already accepted that you belong to both of us. For him to touch you is the same as me touching you. I don't mind."

"Uh-huh, you say that now…And to be straight, I don't *belong* to anyone but myself. No man owns me." Simone left him standing in the driveway and hurried up to the house. She slammed the door behind her with more force than she intended but didn't really care. When she reached her room, she flopped down on the bed and pulled a few sheets of blank paper out of the notebook she kept in her bag. Now was the time to plan her new life in Charlotte. She would get a job and then get a place. If she played her cards right, she wouldn't have to wait too long for it all to work out and she could have some fun all in between.

CHAPTER FOUR

The club was rocking at ten thirty. Simone had brought Artan, but she made it crystal clear that they were not on a date. She was here to have fun, and he was not to get in the way of that. Period. He'd nodded and smiled, but somehow she wasn't so sure he understood what she meant by fun. Not the way she intended to have it.

After she'd downed a tequila shot and sipped half of a vodka and cranberry, she handed him her glass. "Don't put this down, please."

With that, she left him standing there and danced her way to the middle of the floor. She was barely out there before she was surrounded by a small group of men and a few women. Simone laughed and threw her hand in the air. She rocked her hips and worked her way down to the floor in front of one of the men and then came back up. He looked like he was ready to throw her over his shoulder and take her off somewhere. When he danced closer, she held a palm to his chest and then spun to tease the next man. The first man crouched close to her ass but didn't touch.

One of the women sidled up to her. She was white and squat and in no danger of actually finding the beat. Simone liked dancing with women like her because she could get them to do whatever she wanted.

"How do you move your hips like that?" she asked in wonder, trying to emulate Simone.

Simone threw in an extra swerve and shimmied down to the floor again. The woman did the same but came up awkwardly. Simone suppressed a chuckle and then tapped her arm. "How about this?"

She did some zany hand move, and the woman followed. In fact the entire group started doing it. She burst out laughing, and they did too. Well, at least they were having fun. Song after song, she moved without stopping. This was her element.

While she danced facing the woman and another man, they smiled and pointed over her shoulder. Simone glanced back and froze. Artan was behind her. The glass she told him to hold was gone, replaced by a shot glass, which was empty. He moved jerkily, and his eyes were glazed. *Oh hell, he's probably never had alcohol.* Artan was drunk, and if he or someone had bought him a drink, there was no telling how much he had imbibed.

She spun around and jerked the glass from his hand to shove into someone else's hold and then drew him against her. "Okay, crazy, calm down. Just move with me."

He was heavy when he leaned in close to her, almost knocking them both on the floor. His words were slurred. "That d-drinksss wasn't good. Nasty."

"Yeah, I can imagine. You shouldn't have drunk anything I didn't give you."

"Drunkkk," he repeated, grinding his hips into her a little too well. Simone bit her lip.

Somehow she got him moving in a nice rhythm, and she had to admit it felt good being in his arms even if he was plastered. He whispered compliments in her ears, his lips touching her lobe and sending arrows of desire through her more than the words themselves.

"You are so bad," she teased him. His lips moved from her ear to her neck, but she pushed him back with effort. "Whoa, big boy, we're not even going there."

He growled. Simone blinked up at him in surprise. He stared back with dark eyes. In the club lighting, they looked black.

"Did you just growl at me?"

Being so tight in his arms, she felt when something rumbled up through his big chest and ended in his throat. He was growling. "I want you now," he insisted. "This close, with everyone around, I smell it. I can't resist. You understand?"

She understood dude was uninhibited having downed too much alcohol. "Maybe we better go."

He pulled her closer, crushing her to his hard body. Simone winced. His hand moved down to cup her ass, and for the life of her she couldn't pull it off. Artan's other hand slipped up her back, and she felt something giving. A sudden coolness hit her skin that she knew had nothing to do with the fact that she wore a sleeveless minidress. Somehow, Artan had just ripped her dress, and from the look in his eyes, he was prepared to go beyond that right here in the middle of the dance floor.

Panic rose in Simone's chest. She knew how to defend herself. She kept pepper spray in her tiny purse, and she'd kneed more than one man in the nuts in the past. Once, she'd had to use her hand to try twisting them off, but she'd never worried about someone getting the drop on her. Practice with her mother's boyfriends had taught her well. But Artan was different. He was harder and bigger than any man she'd ever been with, and since she couldn't get the tiniest of inches between them, she could do nothing to get him off.

Her hands shook pushing at his chest, but he still didn't budge. "Don't do this, Artan. From what I've seen of you the last few days, I know you don't want to hurt me. Let me go, and we'll leave. Okay?"

He was too far gone. More material tore behind her. She closed her eyes trying to steady herself and think of something. A shout from somewhere nearby caught her attention. She turned her head to look and gasped to see Fallyn barreling through the crowd. He pushed so hard at dancers to get them out of the way, a few fell on the floor. Bouncers were hard on his heels, but he kept moving.

When he drew up to them, one hand was all it took to yank Artan away from her. His fist blurred through the air and smashed into Artan's face. He fell hard on the floor but only shook his head in confusion. Simone stood there holding up her dress, which threatened to fall down. After he'd dealt with his brother, Fallyn swung back to face her and whipped her up into his arms.

The bouncers drew up, and she thought they might have tossed Fallyn out on his ass if he wasn't holding her. But then again, the dead stare he cast their way had the big men skating to a halt holding up their hands.

"Buddy, you need to get your ass out of here before we call the police," one of them threatened.

"And you can leave the girl," the other said.

They thought Fallyn was bullying her instead of it being a rescue. Simone squirmed to get down, but he only clutched her tighter.

"Step aside," he snapped. She felt that same rumble begin in his chest that she'd felt in his twin. *Oh hell.* Was he going to go off and attack her like Artan? She glanced warily up into his eyes and found he was still focused on the men. His eyes were black like Artan's had been, and she knew if Fallyn attacked, it was going to be the bouncers who went flying.

They seemed to come to the same conclusion because they moved out of the way and directed the crowd to do the same. Simone ducked her face into Fallyn's chest, humiliated and embarrassed at what just happened. She'd had boyfriends who fought for her in clubs, and she'd taken a swing or two in the women's bathroom before she learned to control her temper, but she'd never been thrown out of a place.

Outside in the evening air, a truck screeched to a halt, and Simone noticed Blaine behind the wheel. He didn't look happy, and he stepped out. "She okay?"

"Yes," Fallyn said in clipped tones. He finally let her down to her feet, and she had trouble keeping her breasts from bursting free to let the whole world see her goods. Fallyn didn't try to look away from them, but Blaine, apparently immune, took off his jacket and handed it to her. She thrust her arms in the long sleeves and zipped it up. As soon as the clip was beneath her chin, her dress crumpled around her ankles on the ground. To her shame, she burst out crying.

"Dumb, stupid, idiot!" she complained. "Wait till I get my hands on him!"

At the moment, the club door opened, and Artan stepped out. Simone curled her fingers into claws and leaped in his direction, but Fallyn caught her. He dragged her screeching into the truck, and Blaine slipped back into the driver seat.

"You ride in the back," Fallyn told Artan, and Blaine barely gave him enough time to hop in before he sped off toward home.

Simone did her best to get off Fallyn's lap with the ridiculous thought to climb through the small window into the truck's bed to get at Artan, but Fallyn wouldn't let her go. After some time, she calmed down, and then dozed because no one spoke.

Back at Ayana's house, Fallyn let Simone climb out of the truck without holding her back. By then, she wanted nothing more than to shower and to shut herself inside her room. She ignored everybody, including her cousin, and headed upstairs. When she'd stood under the shower until the hot water turned tepid, she stepped out and dried herself. In her room, she followed her nighttime routine because it calmed her mind. First she lotioned her skin, and then she slipped into a T-shirt and a pair of booty shorts. Exhausted, she fell across the bed and was soon fast asleep.

* * * *

In the morning, Simone's mood was no better. She lingered in her room unwilling to face anyone. A knock on the door made her jump.

"What?" she called.

"Hey, can I come in?" Ayana said.

She sighed. "Fine." She went over and flipped the lock. Ayana opened the door and walked in.

"You okay? Blaine and Fallyn told me what happened. Artan is sober now, and he feels like crap for what he did. He wants to come and talk to you, but Fallyn won't let him."

Simone crossed her arms and flopped down on her bed. "I know you're not expecting me to forgive him?"

Ayana held up her hands. "I'm on your side. You're my cousin, and I don't know them. I know you. You like to party, and sometimes you're only thinking of that and nothing else."

"What part of what you said is you being on my side?"

Her cousin sighed and sat down beside her. She took Simone's hand in hers, and they threaded fingers together like they did when they were kids. Simone had spent a lot of time at Ayana's to get away from her mother.

"He'd never had alcohol before. Nobody could know how he would react." Before Simone could defend herself, Ayana put a palm over her lips. "He's sweet and innocent in a way like a little kid. You don't ask a kid to hold your liquor. Whatever you were drinking was sweet, so he didn't say no when someone gave him a couple of shots."

Simone pulled Ayana's hand from her mouth and laughed. "You should have seen the way he danced. It was painful to watch. I wasn't sure if it was his white boy rhythm or it was the fact that he was drunk."

"Probably both," Ayana said, amusement in her eyes.

"I was scared," she admitted. "You know I don't like feeling like that. Hell, I don't let it come over me that often. I get how some of it was my fault. What I don't understand is them. How did Fallyn find me anyway? Wait, never mind." She closed her eyes and shook her head.

"I know a lot has been thrust on you all at once, Simone. I would never have handled it like that, but like Reece told me their situation is a lot different from Reece and Blaine's. It's not fair for them to shove this thing on you as soon as you come here. But family to these people is everything, and they're looking at what amounts to extinction."

"What do you mean?" Simone got how the little family they had left was looking at Artan and Fallyn to continue the line and how much pressure it was for some of them not to have kids when that was what everyone wanted. But in addition to that, she thought Artan leaped before looking. She'd known guys like him, and her uncle, Ayana's father, had called them impulsive. Fallyn wasn't like that. He was more levelheaded. She wondered how often he had to rescue Artan from his stupidity.

Ayana hesitated. "I'm not sure I should say, but you're my cousin, and I don't see any of them explaining all this to you. You have a right to know. Blaine and Reece told me when we were considering become a permanent trio that I should know everything I was getting myself into. And I think you should have that same courtesy.

"Artan and Fallyn are Blaine's cousins, and for whatever reason, their family isn't big. In fact, Blaine thought all his family had died out. There aren't that many males born among them, and I guess that's most important to…what they are. Anyway, Artan and Fallyn are special. Everyone expects them to choose a mate and have babies fast."

"Hm, so in other words, family is pressuring them to get married," Simone said, and Ayana nodded. "Well they can forget about me being the one, because I'm not ready. I don't want to be tied down any time soon."

Ayana agreed. "I hear you. I don't care what their desires are. You shouldn't be rushed. But I do believe in the whole destiny thing now, so just don't write them off yet. Okay? That's your decision, but just talk to Artan. He's devastated at what he tried to do, and he wants to make it up to you."

Simone looked away. She didn't want to give him the time of day. She'd been scared, and she didn't appreciate anyone making her feel that way—drunk or sober. However, she had to admit it was partly her fault. She'd dragged him to the club and then gave him her drink to hold with no explanation.

"Fine, I'll talk to him," she said.

Ayana patted her hand and stood up. "Great, I'll send him up—"

"Oh no. We can go for a walk. I am so not having him alone with me in my room. I'm grown, but we're not going there. Not today." Ayana left her room, and she took her time brushing her teeth and getting dressed for the day. Afterward, she headed downstairs and gestured to Artan as she walked straight toward the door. "I'm going for a walk."

His attention to her every move as she strolled by seemed tinged with depression, and he stood up to follow. When they were outside in the bright sunlight, Artan fell into step beside her. Before she could get two words out, he blurted his apology.

"I'm sorry. I never meant to hurt you." He put out a hand as if to touch her, but she flinched and he drew back. The sorrow in his eyes cut her, and she turned to face the walkway ahead. He went on. "As I mentioned before, many in my family live cut off from civilization. That's no excuse, but I've never had alcohol because of it. I didn't know it would open up my desire for you and I wouldn't be able to hold back."

Simone didn't say a word during his speech. She kept walking giving no indication of whether she accepted his apology or not. In seeming frustration, he reached out to stop her and stood to block her path. Simone tried to pull away, but he held gentle but firm hands at her waist. When she made a small sound of protest, he let go and held his hands up, but he stayed ahead of her so she couldn't get around his big form.

"Forgive me," he whispered.

Simone sighed. "Fine, I forgive you."

A smile broke out on his handsome face like the sun being revealed. "Really?"

"Yes." The way her body stirred with desire for him annoyed her. "It's partly my fault too. I was just thinking about myself and my fun. I shouldn't have dragged you out there."

"No, I had fun. I'd like to do it again," he assured her.

"Yeah I don't know about that." She pursed her lips. "You look big enough not to carry a knife or whatever you used to cut my dress. I don't know if I should go out with your crazy ass again."

Confusion settled on his handsome features, and then his eyebrows went up. The obvious guilt had her hackles up, but she waited for him to explain. He said only, "It wasn't a weapon—not one you would think of." When he stuffed his hands into his pockets and stared at the sky as if he found interest there, all Ayana's anger at him melted. There were things about them that she still didn't know or understand, but Artan wasn't a bad person. That was clear. He didn't make her nervous normally with just his presence like his brother did.

"Okay, we can be friends. Just act like you know, and we'll be fine," she told him.

"Act like I know what?"

She laughed. "Never mind."

She hooked her arm through his, and they continued to walk. By the time, they'd circled the block a few times, Simone had lain her head on his arm and felt comfortable with him again. She mentally searched for what they could do together other than go to the club because she wasn't ready to go down that road with him so soon. And she also needed to thank his brother for rescuing her. She'd forgotten to ask Ayana how Fallyn knew she was in trouble. He probably sniffed them out, but how did he know she needed him right then?

"Hey," she said to Artan.

"Hmm?" He glanced down at her with his usual open and friendly expression.

"Are you and Fallyn connected? Like how did he know I needed him last night? Is it a twin thing? Did he know you were out of control?" Artan seemed to hesitate, and she frowned. "I thought we were friends now. Are you thinking up a lie to tell me?"

That registered surprise on his face. "No, I wouldn't lie to you. I am just wondering if it's best to answer. Blaine said we…or *I* came on too strong even before last night. I don't want to scare you off."

"Just say it," she insisted.

He shrugged. "Fallyn doesn't want to make you his mate."

"That's a relief.

"But he can't help always being aware of you. Whether he likes it or not, your spirit calls to him. He hears you, smells you, and breathes you no matter how hard he fights it. Last night, he must have been half out of his mind because he could smell so many males around you. It was okay for me because I was there and could see, but Fallyn could only sense it and smell it. Then he must have smelled your fear, and that made him come."

Simone walked in silence for a while. How the hell was she supposed to take that? Fallyn smelling the men around her? *Smelling* her fear? What in the world? She had to admit he'd been there when she needed him, but that could have been because he was already somewhere in the club watching them. The way he always had his eyes on her even though he didn't say much showed he was attracted to her. And then there was Blaine screeching up outside with his truck. He might have been around too keeping watch over the twins since they were new.

These people were crazy. Maybe she should get a job and move into her own place. She had some savings. She'd wanted to conserve a little, and Ayana's men stayed in her bed every night, but they had three houses between them. She could ask to rent Blaine's or Reece's place, but she might need a little more distance.

They came back around to Lawnwood Drive and once again Fallyn was chatting with the woman across from Ayana's house. But this time, there was someone else there too and in a whole different class than the frumpy thing from before. This other woman was drop-dead gorgeous with long blonde hair, huge breasts, and a tiny body. All of a sudden, Simone, with all her natural confidence, felt like a dud.

She peeked up at Artan. He watched the threesome with a frown on his face. He probably didn't notice he did it, but he took Simone's hand and started across the street toward his brother. "Fallyn, why are you talking to them?" Artan demanded. Simone's eyes widened. *Bold isn't he?*

Fallyn looked away from the sexy woman, and his eyes met Simone's. She couldn't read a thing from him except anger, but then his eyes swept her from head to foot. He peered at her so long, the blonde turned to see who he was looking at. The displeasure in her was not hidden in the least.

"So, Fallyn, my brother and I can expect you at our little dinner party, right?" she said, ignoring both Artan and Simone.

"And I'll be there," the other woman said. She circled around Fallyn to sidle up to Artan and held out her hand as if she expected him to kiss it. "I'm Brooke. You must be Fallyn's brother. You two look exactly alike. And this is my friend Abby."

"Artan," he muttered and shook Brooke's hand in a rough pump. She winced and then noticed that he still held Simone's hand at his side.

"Oh, are you two a couple?" she said and stepped back to link her arm through Fallyn's. "That's so cute." Her stance indicated she and Fallyn were too, but Simone picked up on Abby's irritation. How long Brooke thought they were going to be friends she didn't know, but if Fallyn were in the market for a woman, Abby would probably be it. She could feed all his children with those boobs—unless they weren't real. But they looked it, and she'd seen plenty of fake ones in New York.

"We're all three—" Artan began, but she jerked his arm.

"Come on, Artan. I'm ready for breakfast now," Simone told him. "I think in all this sun if I don't get something in my stomach soon, I'm going to pass out. Man, it's hot in the South."

She only said it to get him going and to keep him from saying what she knew he was about to say, that she, he, and Fallyn were all three in a relationship. The man didn't give up, and he couldn't decide for his brother or for her who they chose to see. But her words about being ill had a greater affect than she expected. Fallyn and Artan both snapped to attention. Fallyn was at her side with even more annoyance on his handsome face.

"You should not have come out if you hadn't eaten." He excused himself from Brooke and Abby with a nod and walked with her and Artan down the street and to the opposite side to Ayana's house. Talk about attentive, she thought with pleasure. She didn't look back as they entered the house, but she already knew she'd made two new enemies, and the game she never meant to play was on.

CHAPTER FIVE

"I can't believe she invited me," Simone said as she checked her makeup one last time in Ayana's bedroom mirror.

"Not like she could exclude you when she invited all of us," her cousin responded. "Besides, Mark has been after Blaine to do some side jobs during the summer. He will do everything he can not to offend him. I don't know why Blaine has been putting him off. He didn't even want to go until I convinced him. I need to get out of the house. Of course, Abby likes to act all high sedity. Her brother seems nice, but she gets on my nerves sometimes. Reece agreed with me that we should go, and Blaine gave in." She shrugged.

Simone thought about the many times she'd watched her cousin do whatever her lovers told her, so the fact that she pushed for something Blaine didn't want surprised her. "Do you always obey them?"

"Please, it's not about obedience. They'd do anything for me, and I like to do the same."

"But you have to admit your boyfriends are really dominant."

Ayana flushed as she applied lipstick to her lips. "Yeah, they are, and it turns me on. Don't tell them that though. I fuss and all that, but I love how they treat me like I'm special. I don't get to carry one bag for myself or lift heavy stuff. If they're taking too long to fix something around the house, all I do is act like I'm about to do it, and they flip out. You'd think a hammer would bruise my hand just holding it the way they act. I love it!"

Simone watched the joy in her cousin's eyes and felt a twinge of jealousy. She was happy for Ayana, but she couldn't imagine living her life like that. She'd always taken care of everything, including her mother when she didn't have a loser boyfriend. "I don't think Artan's that way."

Ayana grinned. "Oh, it's like that?"

"No," Simone shrieked and then calmed herself. "I was just making an observation. What he is or isn't has nothing to do with me."

"Uh huh." Disbelief colored Ayana's expression. "Well, I think you just haven't seen him in the right circumstances. They're all the same."

"Whatever. I guess you're talking about that shifter thing again. I haven't seen anyone show me evidence."

"Trust me. You don't want to see evidence until or if you start feeling something for them other than just attraction. You'd be on the next bus out of here if you do before then."

Simone sighed. She walked over to the bed and picked up her purse. She'd opted for a small black one that was little more than a wallet to match her black dress. Abby had actually insisted that they dress somewhat elegantly for a home dinner party. Here they had been gathering in the back yard around a grill in shorts and flip-flops all this time, and she wanted to eat inside. Whatever made some people feel good, she guessed.

"So how am I going to not think all y'all are crazy in the South if I don't see something real?" she asked.

"Go with your instincts. Now let's get moving before Blaine or Reece follow through with their threat and come up here and carry me downstairs."

Simone pursed her lips. "Yeah, you'd hate that!"

They headed down the stairs with Simone behind Ayana. Simone watched as Reece held his hands up and caught Ayana at the end of the steps to lift her down into his arms. The two of them stood crushed against each other with Reece devouring her lips in a hungry kiss. As soon as he released her, Blaine whipped Ayana into his arms for a repeat. Simone held the banister in a tight grip and squeezed her legs together while waiting for them to move out of the way. They were a horny trio and just watching how the guys grabbed freely at Ayana's ass made Simone hot for her own lover.

She realized her desire must have gotten her a little wet when both Fallyn and Artan appeared at the bottom of the steps. Both men's eyes were locked on her bare legs, and she felt like they could see straight up to her red thong even though common sense told her they couldn't. As Simone descended the steps, she wondered if they would have the same animal hunger if they scented Abby's or Brooke's desire. The thought of it was gross, but she found herself hoping their reaction was only for her. That was selfish since she wasn't trying to have a relationship with either one, but she couldn't help herself.

When she moved off the last step, Artan was there to wrap an arm around her waist. Even with four-inch slingbacks on her feet, she wasn't nearly as tall as he was. She felt feminine and small, which was nice. He moved in as if to kiss her, but she turned her head. He landed on her cheek. She would not be refreshing her lipstick this soon like Ayana was already doing. Besides, they were not dating.

At Abby and Mark's house, soft music was playing when they walked in. Scented candles flickered their light and scent from elegant side tables cornering the couch and loveseat. The layout was similar to Ayana's place, having a large living room and kitchen occupying one side of the house. A hall led to a bathroom and what Simone assumed was bedrooms. She liked Ayana's place better, having two floors.

Abby floated into the living room looking like royalty in her bearing and a model in the form-fitting all white dress that had no sleeves and stopped just beneath her cootchie. Simone would never have been so bold if she had boobs that big, and the way Abby bounced about greeting her guests, Simone thought she was in serious danger of flashing them all.

"Simone," she said coolly when she got to her.

"Abby," Simone echoed. "Thanks for inviting me."

Abby's look said she didn't, and she went on around the group. Although there were several people there that Simone didn't know, Abby hooked on to Fallyn and ignored them. Brooke of all people handed around hors d'oeuvres and took drink orders that Mark made. Abby cornered Fallyn at the end of the couch and lowered her head close to his as they spoke in quiet tones. Simone ground her teeth until she reminded herself that Fallyn could do what the hell he wanted to.

She found Mark at the kitchen counter stirring drinks. "Hey, I'm Simone, Ayana's cousin," she said.

He smiled. The man was as hot as Abby was beautiful. They must have incredible genes. His green eyes were clear and friendly, and rather than blond hair tumbling over his forehead, it was deep brown, making Simone wonder if Abby had found her color in a bottle.

"Hi, I'm Mark. Abby's brother. Good to meet you."

She leaned an elbow on the counter. "If you're taking orders, I'd love a hurricane. Know how to make it?"

"Vodka uh rum…" he began.

She laughed. "Scootch over. Let me show you how it's done." They chitchatted while she mixed a big picture of the drink and let him test a bit. At his proclamation that it was good, she winked and went back to tweaking it a little more. When she glanced over at him, she found he was eying her ass, and she grinned. Maybe this party wouldn't be so bad.

Out of the blue, he reached over and ran a light finger along her arm. "Are you seeing anyone?"

"Yes, she is," came a hard reply.

Simone's eyes grew wide when she turned around to find Artan standing there. The sweet, friendly man she'd been used to was gone, and if she didn't know that he'd worn a sky blue collared shirt to Fallyn's white one, she would have sworn it was his brother. The scowl on his face made him look exactly like Fallyn.

He walked over and nipped Simone away from Mark's side, causing her to crash into his chest. The liquid in the glass she'd been holding to sample her hurricane sloshed over the side and plopped on the floor. "Artan!" she grumbled.

"It's fine," Mark said. "I got it." He tore off a paper towel from a roll on the counter and wiped up the spill, and Simone glared at Artan. He didn't appear sorry.

"He doesn't get to touch you," Artan growled in her ear.

She struggled to push him back, but he wasn't letting go. "We're not seeing each other, so you need to calm down. Who I let touch me is none of your business. Let me go."

"Are you okay, Simone?" Mark asked.

The atmosphere in the kitchen had gone from friendly to hostile in a matter of seconds. Didn't this fool Artan know Mark could toss him out of his house? Then how would he stop him from touching her? But from the look in Artan's eyes, she didn't think he would go without a fight, and definitely not without her.

While they stood there in a sort of face off, Fallyn walked in. His cool eyes assessed the situation. "Go out there, Artan." He pointed toward the living room.

Artan seemed about to argue, but he released Simone and left her closer to Fallyn than to Mark. She guessed he left only because he expected Fallyn to act like he did, all possessive and stupid. When would he get through his head his twin didn't want her? Thinking about it, she shook her head in annoyance at herself. The more she reasserted the fact, the more she wondered if it bothered her that he didn't want her. Her ego wasn't so big that she thought every man should fall at her feet, so why care if Fallyn didn't?

Fallyn glanced at Mark. "Give us a minute." The words were a command. The dude was tossing Mark out of his own kitchen. Simone bristled, and when Mark did like he was told, she started to follow, but

Fallyn moved to block her path. “Wait.”

She glared up at him and put her hands on her hips. “You can boss around your brother and Mark, but you’re not going to tell me where I can and can’t go. Get out of my way.”

He didn’t move a muscle. Simone considered shoving by him, but if he was determined to keep her where she was, she didn’t think she was going anywhere. Over his shoulder, she heard the others laughing and chatting. Brooke’s purring voice reached her, and she almost laughed realizing the woman was coming on to Artan. Simone wasn’t bothered in the least. Artan had made his dislike of her clear.

“You know Artan and Fallyn are my cousins,” Blaine was saying. Brooke’s throaty response went to a squeak which sounded a lot like fear. What was that about? Simone couldn’t focus on whether someone gave an explanation of her reaction because Fallyn took that moment to raise her chin and force her to look at him.

“You cannot play games with my brother,” he said.

She sucked her teeth. “Who’s playing games? I don’t belong to him.”

He released her chin and drew her closer to his chest with his hands on her waist. “He has claimed you as his mate, and he cannot tolerate you with another man in his presence. It is dangerous.”

“Are you threatening me, ’cause I’m not the one,” she snapped. She believed him when he said it was dangerous. Hell, just looking at them, she saw something wild and animal-like. That didn’t mean she believed their crazy shifter story though.

Fallyn frowned. “Of course not. *You* would never be hurt.”

“Meaning Artan will bully any man I talk to.”

He sighed. “This is why…” He broke off what he was about to say, but she could guess what he was about to say. She didn’t understand them and probably never would. Fallyn looked out for her because he was concerned about his brother. “Do not provoke him. That is all I ask.”

Simone had had enough. She poked him in the chest. “I will do exactly what I want to do. If Artan can't handle me talking to other men, that's his problem. Like I said, we're not dating. Now, if you'll excuse me, I'm going back to the party to have a good time."

She stepped away from him, grabbed the picture with one of her favorite drinks in it, and went back to the living room. She poured hurricanes for those who wanted it, and topped off hers too. She smiled and laughed, and when someone turned on a song she could move to, she danced the night away. Not one time, did she bother with what Abby was doing. The woman had wrapped herself around Fallyn's arm and ignored the rest of her guests to talk to him. Artan brooded in the corner, and Simone dragged Mark to the middle of the floor to dance with her. Brooke seemed to have written off the twins as potential bed partners, and poor Mark found himself a sandwich between the two of them as Brooke, soused, shimmied behind him.

"I don't think he's very happy," Mark told her. He pretended not to care that Artan's gaze never left them from his spot in the corner, but he had been careful not to touch her.

"Doesn't matter to me," she said and gave him a wink. When the buzz from her drink wasn't enough, she poured another. She spun so that her back was to Mark and danced in close to him. His hands hovered above her hips. "Chicken," she teased.

He groaned.

"How about we go for a walk," she suggested. "It's hot in here."

"Sure."

They didn't give an explanation but left the party. Once she'd slammed the door behind them, she grabbed his hand, and they ran down the drive to the street. She didn't stop until they were halfway down the dark road. Since there were so few streetlights, there were plenty of patches where visibility was almost nil. A person had to take a step on faith and hope not to break one's neck in the process. At least if Artan came out, he wouldn't see where they'd gone.

"Mm, I love it here," she said as she breathed in the night air.

She expected Mark to respond to her comment, but instead, he stared at her face. "You're very beautiful. You like playing men against each other, don't you?"

Simone frowned. "Excuse me? How was I playing anyone?"

He shrugged. "Three men wanting you, all vying for your attention."

She stopped walking. "Two! And for your information, I didn't ask for any of it. I asked you if you knew how to make a hurricane, and the next thing I know you're running your fingers up my arms. And I'm the blame for that?"

"I'm sorry."

"Whatever." She started to walk away, but he caught her arm to pull her back. He encircled her waist and drew her against his chest. She waited for desire to kick in, maybe a little wetting of her panties like what happened whenever Artan or even Fallyn touched her. Nothing.

Mark leaned in and kissed her cheek. When she didn't protest, he moved to her neck and took a light nibble there. "You smell incredible. I could eat you up."

"Is that right?" Maybe she needed to get into it more. Listening to her cousin with her lovers had made her so horny for some action, and now with Mark obviously offering it, she was going all prudish. She raised her hands to his chest and felt his hard muscles. He had a great body, and he smelled good too. She couldn't identify the cologne, but it was familiar, and it usually made her all melty for a sexy man. Mark so wasn't doing it for her. Maybe it was because she was worried Artan was going to jump out from somewhere or Fallyn.

"Yeah, I could," Mark continued. "I've never fucked a black woman before, but I've always fantasized about it."

And that was the cold bucket of water dumped on her head. If she'd felt nothing before, she definitely didn't feel it now. She wiggled to get out of his arms, but he wasn't ready to let go. "That's sweet, but I don't go for being the fulfillment of that kind of fantasy. I date guys who've been there and know they prefer a black woman."

His lips tightened. "You think those twins have? You'd be an exotic treat for them too."

"It's different with them." She didn't know how she knew, but she was sure it wasn't about skin color with Fallyn and Artan. Maybe it was what Ayana had told her that made her sure. "Look, I have to go. It's late."

"Come on," he coaxed. "Let's go back to your place and have some fun. They're all going to be at the party for a while, I bet."

"No, I don't think so." She gave him a push. One of his hands on her waist moved down and around to her ass to squeeze. Simone reacted without thinking. She kneed him in the nuts. He bent in half with a cry of pain.

"You bitch!" he growled. Gone was the nice neighbor, and the bastard came out strong and unmistakable. Simone rolled her eyes and spun away to go back up the street. But Mark caught her wrist. He jerked her to him. "Oh no you don't."

Fear clogged her throat with a lump. She struggled in his hold. There wasn't a soul out there in the darkness, and if he wanted to, Mark could rape her and no one would be the wiser until it was over. But before he could do more than take a breath, he was flat on his back in the street. Artan shoved a forearm into Mark's neck, cutting off his air. Mark flopped about gasping and struggling to push Artan away. His punches, which looked hard to Simone, seemed to graze off Artan's chest, and Mark winced as if it hurt him with each blow.

Simone grabbed Artan's shoulder. "Artan, stop. You're killing him. He's not worth it. Let go!" He didn't listen. The low growl in his throat vibrated through his back and she wrapped her arms around his neck to try pulling him. "Artan!" she screamed into his ear.

Someone else came up behind her and plucked her off Artan. She looked up to see that it was Fallyn. He got between the two men. Simone expected him to be the voice of reason, but Fallyn dragged Mark off the ground and dangled him by the front of his shirt. Fallyn's other hand was balled into a fist.

She gasped. "What the hell has gotten into you two? Stop!"

"He kissed you," Fallyn accused her.

"You were watching? I thought you didn't give a crap." She closed her eyes and shook her head. "You know what, do what you want. I'm leaving, but if you or Artan lay one hand on him, I'm never speaking to either of you again."

She turned hearing Mark yelp in pain as Fallyn dropped him like a hot potato. Fallyn murmured something that sounded threatening to Mark, and the two of them followed her down the street toward Ayana's house. She let herself in with the key Ayana had given her. She half expected Blaine and the others to be there, but the house was dark. The others hadn't left the party.

Simone went straight to her room, ignoring Fallyn and Artan. She shed her clothes and then took a shower. By the time she was in her nightie, the happy buzz she'd had earlier was long gone, and she grumbled. "Stupid idiots."

She lay back and threw an arm over her head. Sleep was not coming any time soon. Replaying the scene outside, she was grateful that Artan and Fallyn had come, but they'd done it because Artan thought she was his. She didn't even know the man. Sure she was attracted to him, and in a way, it turned her on to have such an Alpha guy protecting her. But what if she was really into Mark? What if he wasn't a jerk and wasn't trying to force himself on her? What then? Would Artan have still attacked him?

A knock sounded at her door. She hadn't heard Ayana come back, so she knew it was one of the twins. This time she made sure her nightie was covered with the robe she'd bought recently. "Yeah?" she said to Artan when she opened the door to find him and his brother there.

"We're sorry," he said. "*I'm* sorry. I don't want you to be afraid of me."

"I'm not," she admitted. "I think you went overboard. I think you're way too possessive of me when I'm not your girlfriend. I get that you need to find someone to marry and all that, but I don't appreciate you signing me up for it without my permission."

He looked down tapping his thumb against his thigh. He was dressed only a pair of shorts, and his hair was wet from a shower. He looked so good, and just from a glimpse alone she could tell his muscles were a whole lot harder than Mark's. She tried not to notice too much, but both men's eyes had gone darker as soon as she did. *My scent.* She groaned. They were unnatural.

Fallyn elbowed past his brother, but he didn't make a move to come into her room. "I think that you have some interest in my brother. You do not understand our ways, and I believe if you give him a chance to know you better and him you, you will not regret it."

"You're his lawyer?" She pursed her lips. If she expected Fallyn to apologize for how he behaved, she'd probably be waiting an eternity. His words were coaxing but his bearing told her "I warned you." She sighed. "Fine. He can take me out on one date. If he acts stupid, I'm out."

Artan darted forward and raised her fingers to his lips. One kiss of her fingertips made her squeeze her legs together. As if a cool breeze had swept through the house, her nipples hardened. The robe was no barrier to disguise it as both men raked her body with their hot gazes. She felt naked, and desire made goose bumps prickle her skin.

"I will come too," Fallyn announced.

When had she become sandwiched between them? Either way, she didn't want to move from there. Fallyn was so close behind her, she felt his warm breath on her neck—a whole different reaction from when Mark's mouth was there. Artan had released her hands to skim her hips in a light caress. She caught her breath looking up at him, and then his mouth descended on hers. The man didn't hesitate for a second. His tongue filled her mouth. He growled hungrily as he devoured her. She was weak under the onslaught, swaying until she had to catch herself with palms to his hard chest.

Not to be outdone, Fallyn turned her head from his brother to claim her mouth as well. He wasn't interested in her that way. Why did he push his tongue into her mouth? Who the hell cared? She gave into it and shivered when she felt his rigid cock pressed into her back.

Fallyn's mouth moved from her lips to her neck, and he sucked the place where Mark had nibbled. He pulled so hard on her skin, she was sure she'd have a hickey there tomorrow. Artan pushed in closer. As if they signaled each other in silence, Fallyn gripped her hips and raised her a little. Her legs spread of their own accord, and Artan stepped between them. His cock was hard too, and it brushed her now-swollen clit. Only the material of his shorts kept him from gliding into her pussy, because she was soaked. Fallyn dipped his knees and spooned her ass.

She moaned. "What are y'all doing to me?"

She was seconds from giving herself fully to them when Fallyn drew back and pushed at his brother's chest. "No, we've given our word. We will do it like Blaine said."

Artan seemed more far gone than his twin. His eyes were coal black, and his breathing was ragged. She thought he clamped sharp teeth together, but wasn't sure. He nodded but didn't say a word as he let her legs down. Simone toppled sideways a little, but both men caught her and held her steady until her head cleared. Where all that had come from she didn't know. Pulling herself together, she ran the back of her hand across her swollen lips and looked from one to the other.

With a deep breath, she said, "Tomorrow night."

They agreed and left her room with obvious reluctance. Simone shut the door behind them and locked it. Partly to keep them out and a whole lot to keep herself inside. She didn't know where the date would go, but she was beginning to wonder if a chaste little date was what she really wanted.

CHAPTER SIX

"I can't believe you're going out with them after last night," Ayana said. "I would have been pissed. But Mark did deserve it acting like he did. I never would have thought it about him. Not that I knew him that well. Blaine's ticked."

Simone sat still while Ayana styled her hair. Her cousin was rambling, and she appeared more upset than Simone now that she'd had a chance to sleep on the situation. Then again, since Blaine wasn't happy, the woman who loved him wasn't. Simone wondered if Blaine had sensed Mark wasn't a good man and that was why he didn't want to go to his house. She knew one thing. There wouldn't be any side jobs for him. She knew that Blaine had taken Artan and Fallyn out that morning to talk to them.

"What was up with Brooke's reaction in learning that they're related to Blaine? She got a thing against him or what?"

Ayana blinked at the sudden change in conversation. "Oh that. She knows they're not quite…human. She doesn't know the details, but they had a sort of run in last year, and let's just say she doesn't try to come on to Blaine or Reece. Knowing Artan and Fallyn are the same probably freaked her out."

So it was the shifter thing again, and Brooke knew about it. Or from the sound of it not the details. She knew enough to be afraid. Simone recalled how their eyes changed when they were sexually excited. She thought the same happened when they were angry too but couldn't remember. Some white people's eye colors deepened in response to their emotions, but she didn't know if the extreme the twins' did was normal.

"What happened?" she asked. "Did they shift in front of her?"

Ayana frowned at her in the mirror. "You still don't believe it, do you?"

"I believe," she lied.

Ayana laughed. "Whatever. It's all null and void if things don't work out between the three of you. I'll leave it to Artan or Fallyn to tell you more. Well, your hair is done. With that and your outfit, they'll be falling all over you."

Simone stood up and gave her a quick hug. "Girl, please, I could go out there naked and they'd be all over me."

Ayana snorted. "If you went out there naked, you'd never get out of the house. All of their sex drives are out of control. Okay, have a good time, and you've got my number and the guys' numbers if you need them."

"Yep. Thanks."

Tonight Simone wore a purple sleeveless dress with beaded strap that came up just above her breasts and went around her neck. From her bustline down to the upper part of her thighs, it billowed and would flare out if she spun in a circle. She matched the outfit with strappy silver heels and silver jewelry. As soon as she came down the stairs, both Artan and Fallyn popped to their feet in the living room and stared at her. Fallyn was the first to snap out of his trance, and he moved across the room to take her hand. Well they might have been raised in the wilderness, but they had some manners.

Warmth spread throughout her system, and she smiled up at him through lashes coated with mascara to make them look fuller. If she wondered whether men could be captured with a woman's eyes alone, she didn't question it any longer. Fallyn looked lost as if she'd cast a spell. Simone couldn't remember ever feeling so powerful or attractive with a man. Of course she liked when they appeared to enjoy the sight, but

Fallyn's reaction had her heart pounding. And when Artan joined him at her side, her breath caught in her chest.

Reece strolled into the room wiping his hands on a dish towel. "Wow, Simone, you look great." He'd said it casually with no hint of flirting, but both her dates gave low, rumbling growls of warning. Reece only laughed and held up his hands. "Down, guys. I have my own mate, and I'm happy with her."

"Thanks," Simone murmured to Reece's compliment and then glided out the front door. A thrill of excitement hit her knowing Artan and Fallyn came tumbling after. Neither of them drove and for some reason, she'd never bothered to learn herself. Blaine volunteered to take them, and he was waiting in Reece's SUV.

Artan opened the back door for her, and she slipped inside. He followed her in, and Fallyn went around to the other side. She hid another smile that they were all three treating poor Blaine like a chauffeur, but he didn't seem to mind. "The Nocturnal it is," he announced.

When they had bid Blaine good night and climbed up the steep steps to the Epicentre leading to the Nocturnal restaurant, she paused to admire her dates. "Y'all have adjusted fast. I mean you wear those slacks, dress shirts, and shoes like you were born in them."

Her words triggered Fallyn to tug at the collar of his shirt in discomfort, while Artan grinned. "If you like it, I do too," he told her. She had the feeling he could care less. Artan was the freest of all of them. Whether clothed or unclothed, he was fine.

"I like whatever you wear," she assured him, and infused lots of meaning in the words. His gaze grew intense, and she walked ahead of him.

Several men tried catching her eye, but she ignored all of them. Who could compare to the sexy guys she was with tonight? And she'd promised to give them a chance. Tonight would be fun. She loved the atmosphere in this restaurant even though Ayana and her boyfriends had only brought them once. The food was great, although she wondered if it would be enough for the twins. Ayana had told her Reece and Blaine had left the place and stopped at Cook Out for more food. Their stomachs were bottomless pits according to her, so the Nocturnal was her pleasure, not theirs.

When they were settled at their table, Simone flipped open the menu to see what she wanted, but Artan and Fallyn didn't bother. She frowned. "Hey, I know y'all are eating right? See what you want."

"That's not necessary," Fallyn told her. "We will order steak—rare—and salad."

She rolled her eyes and laughed. "Should have known. Gah, rare. Well have at it." When she learned they didn't have any cod to her disappointment, Simone ordered grilled duck breast served with roasted sweet potatoes. For a drink she went with a Liquid Sunshine since she wasn't a fan of wine. Fallyn and Artan stuck with water.

"So," Simone began when the waitress left them, "tell me about your family and your home and all. I want to know more."

Fallyn eyed her as if to judge whether she really wanted to know, and then he fingered the cloth napkin. Neither of them had unfolded it, but Simone had hers in her lap. "We come from a small clan I guess you could call it. Not more than twenty of us all together. There are few males, and many of the men have several mates."

Simone blinked. She wanted to stop him right there, but pressed her lips together. If she got an attitude now Fallyn might go back to being angry at her saying she would never understand. So she kept quiet.

"For some reason, our women have trouble conceiving. There were quite a few miscarriages and a couple stillborns in the last seasons." She gasped, and hearing the pain in his voice, which he quickly masked, she laid a hand on his. Fallyn allowed her comforting touch for a moment and then pulled away. His expression was one of hard anger. Simone glanced at Artan. He too was affected remembering, but hid it right away. She wanted to ask if either of them had lost children, but hesitated. Then she changed her mind. If they had "mates" back home, they shouldn't be sniffing around her. She wasn't one of them, and if Fallyn didn't like it, well it only reinforced what he thought anyway.

"Do you or Artan have…uh…girlfriends back in South Carolina?" She couldn't bring herself to say *mates*. It seemed too biblical or animal-like.

"No, not at this time," Fallyn said.

"So you never had kids?"

Artan shook his head. "No, if we did that would mean we had a mate. We do not have children outside of a bonding."

"Oh, excuse me," she said with sarcasm. Where she came from it was a common occurrence. Not that she'd ever been pregnant. The jury was out on whether she even wanted them. She liked children fine, but no man had been perfect enough or made her love him enough to want his kids. She kept thinking about dealing with someone she hated until her child was eighteen, and it scared her. Not to mention the wonderful example her parents had given her on the subject.

Artan reached out and stroked her cheek. She let him, enjoying the warm touch of his palm. They were both already so different from any man she'd ever dated, and she found herself hoping being here wouldn't change them too much. She kind of liked them wild and innocent yet strong and fierce. Now that Fallyn wasn't frowning, the two of them looked exactly alike. But she thought she could tell them apart anyway.

"What about you?" Fallyn asked, interrupting her thoughts. "Have you ever had a…" He searched for the right word. "Husband. No, boyfriend."

She laughed. "Uh, yeah I've had plenty of boyfriends." The twins frowned at her, and she figured if any of those men were here now, they'd pummel him into the ground. "Not like *that*. I've dated a lot, but I'm not a total slut. I go out, like we're doing now. It's not a big deal. I've never been married, not even close, which is probably sad."

She turned serious and looked away from their inquisitive eyes. "My mother likes to get boyfriends that support her. Well, somewhat. And they weren't always the best men to be around." She shrugged. "Most of the time, she and I did okay together. She did her thing, and I did mine. But her latest man wanted us both, and I wasn't having it. She blamed me. We argued. So here I am. Starting over, I guess."

To her surprise, Fallyn laced his fingers with hers, and then Artan followed suit. Fallyn rubbed his thumb across her skin, and shivers of pleasure zinged through her. "You say it like it does not bother you. But I sense pain. You expected her to protect you as a mother should with her cub."

Simone grinned. "Yeah, cub. Well, I'm grown. I can look after myself."

Artan frowned and squeezed her hand a little. "She should have protected you from this man. Who is he? Fallyn and I can—"

"Whoa, boy." She laughed. "That's sweet and all, but I got it. It's all water under the bridge. I have that job waitressing. I'll be starting on Monday, so I think I'll be good."

He examined her face as if to see if she was sure. "We can care for you."

"It's fine."

After they had finished their meal, Simone pulled her wallet out. "I figure we can go Dutch."

"Dutch?" they echoed together.

"Yeah, you know. I pay half the bill, and you two can take half. Or I guess we can do three ways, but you'd said your people share everything."

Fallyn pushed her hand away when she tried laying cash on the table. He pulled out a wallet she didn't know he had. Somehow she'd thought they wouldn't know what money was. She gaped when Fallyn flipped his wallet open and she caught sight of a thick wad of bills. He peeled off two fiftys.

"Damn, why are you carrying that kind of money." She wrinkled her nose. “And I thought you two were poor. Did Blaine give it to you?”

They both looked insulted, but Artan spoke up. “We are not poor. Our people own the land we live on, and it produces for us in multiple ways. We live on the bare necessities as I told you, but it’s not because we can’t afford more.”

She stood up as Fallyn settled the entire check. “I’m sorry. I shouldn’t have assumed.

“It’s fine,” Fallyn told her. He stuffed his thick wallet back into his pocket and took her hand. They led her out of the dim interior of the restaurant. As they left, several women tossed her envious looks, and she glanced again at her dates. They were both well over six feet with muscular builds. Their dark hair hung to their shoulders, and they appeared so rugged and strong, it was easy to believe they’d just run in from the wild.

She took hold of their arms and walked between them as they returned to street level. Night had fallen, and some people were already drunk and staggering along the walk. A couple of attendants were hailing taxis for those who needed them, but Simone wanted to enjoy uptown Charlotte for a little while longer.

“Should we walk?” she asked.

“Sure,” they said.

At the corner, they stopped for oncoming traffic to go by. A black man yelled out to her, “Hey, sista, drop those white boys and come with me.”

She rolled her eyes, and when both Fallyn and Artan tried to go after him, she squeezed their thick biceps to hold onto them. They were each frowning, and she grinned. “Dudes, it’s not a crime for him to yell out comments.”

“It is disrespectful of you,” Fallyn complained.

She shrugged. “That’s how they are. No big deal.”

But Fallyn didn’t seem to like the noise even though she considered it way tame, clean, and just nice compared to back home. When his agitation grew, she wondered how they'd ever really connect long term. She was a city girl, and he wanted to go back to nature. In fact, she wondered what kept him here this long.

"Maybe we should get out of here," she suggested.

Fallyn sighed in relief. "We will take you to a place we discovered here. There's a lake and trees."

They hailed a taxi, and Simone twitched all the way there as Fallyn guided the driver in the direction to go. The way he watched the road with such an intent concentration, she wondered how he knew. Artan at her side leaned close to her ear and whispered, "He's scenting the way."

She shook her head. "Again with the smelling thing."

"You won't believe until you see," he said. She shrugged, but he didn't say anymore.

When they turned onto a narrow road, she smelled the water. The air was clean, and trees were everywhere. She flinched at the readout for the cost of the trip. Fallyn had had to pay a good amount down in order for the man to come this far. She didn't blame him, but he paid the fare, and she pulled off an extra bill for a tip from the money in his hand to give the driver. He made no comment.

After the taxi disappeared, she frowned. "Now I'm wondering how we'll get home."

"Don't worry." Artan took her hand.

She got him to wait while she pulled off her shoes and held them in one hand. Then they walked down toward the water. A warm breeze swept in stirring her hair, and she drew in a deep breath while looking up at the moon. "We probably shouldn't be here."

"Do you want to leave?" Fallyn strolled up behind her and rested his hands on her waist. He drew her back to his broad chest, and she rested there. Desire coiled through her insides, but she didn't resist it as she'd done before. Both men seemed to become more alert in some way. They knew every time when she got excited. The experience was both disturbing and exciting.

"No."

Fallyn leaned down and nuzzled her neck. His touch reminded her of Ayana's and her boyfriends' reactions at seeing the hickey on her neck that next morning after the party. Reece had been amused. Ayana looked worried, and Blaine frowned. She'd half expected him to take the guys off for another lecture like their big brother, but he hadn't said a word. For a while, she'd been disturbed thinking Blaine and Reece would just know if she'd had sex with them, but since it never happened anyway, she'd eventually calmed down about it.

"Do you want to sit down?" Artan asked.

She peered at the ground and wrinkled her nose. "There might be bugs or worms down there. At night it creeps me out."

Fallyn wasn't happy about that, but he dropped down to the thick grass without a word and held out his hand to her. Simone bit her lip. She slipped her fingers into his, and he pulled her gently onto his lap. If desire had sparked in her before, it flamed to a roaring fire with her planted smack in the middle of his crotch, his hard thighs beneath hers, and her back leaning on his chest. Fallyn brought his arms up around her to hold her tight to him, and she didn't miss the stiff shifting beneath her ass.

He turned her head and captured her mouth in a hungry kiss. She tilted her head back, allowing him full access. His low groan made her nipples peak, drawing his palm down to cup one of her breasts. A shudder of pleasure passed through her when he pinched the tiny bud, and she broke off the kiss. "This isn't the way I expected the date to go."

"Do you want me to stop?" He looked into her eyes. For the life of her, she couldn't find a reason to say yes.

Artan took the spot next to them and leaned in for a kiss of his own. She couldn't bring herself to deny him what she'd given to his brother. And why would she want to? They were expert kissers. She'd had lovers she had to teach, men who would clench their mouths so tight, it felt like a battle just to kiss. Artan and Fallyn were naturals. First one devoured her mouth and then the other. They tag teamed her, each matching the assault on her lips with caresses that had her panties soaked through. And the wetter she got, the more it seemed to excite them. She grew dizzy with their loving and had to rest against Fallyn while she caught her breath.

"Oh wow," she rasped, fanning herself as she tried getting more comfortable on Fallyn's lap. "Y'all got me all worked up." She felt that Fallyn was rock hard and glanced over at Artan. The crotch of his pants was tented, and there was a distinct imprint of his length going to one side. Her mouth watered, and she licked her lips.

She raised her gaze from his pants to his face. His eyes weren't clearly visible even with the moon illuminating the area, but she bet they were as dark as the night. "You're wet," he said and rested a hand at the top of her thigh.

Her dress had risen when she sat down. Not that it had far to go given the thing was short. Artan inched it higher to reveal her thong. His fingertips grazed the strip of material, and she moaned. "Artan."

"Let me taste you," he whispered.

She shivered. Nerves clenched her stomach muscles, but the thought of him licking her pussy turned her on even more. Beneath her, Fallyn's cock twitched. She guessed the suggestion got him hotter too.

When she said nothing, Artan bent over and kissed her pussy through her panties. He breathed her essence, and she had to bite off another moan. "I want to please you, Simone. I can smell your want, and it's driving me crazy."

She recalled that first night she arrived and how they'd stood outside her bedroom door. She had thought they were turned on by the sounds Ayana was making, but their attention had been wholly on her. That was the hottest experience of her life so far, just knowing they were tormented because they smelled her desire. It was unbelievable but such a turn-on.

"Yes," she breathed. "I want it."

Fallyn untied the strap around her neck, and Artan dragged down the front of her dress to let her breasts free. The cool night air stirred over her skin bringing her nipples to a rigid point. Artan squeezed one breast and bent over to suck a nipple. She moaned. Her head went back, and Fallyn captured her chin to make her kiss him. He'd not taken more than a few hungry tastes before Artan pulled her mouth from his brother and kissed her too. Back and forth, they shared her, and Simone felt like she was going to come from that alone.

When Artan raised his head, she braced herself on Fallyn and moved her ass over his crotch. He growled, his eyes flicking closed. "Take her panties off," he commanded of his brother.

Artan lifted one of her thighs and worked the thin material down then moved to the other side. He flung the thong aside and then spread her legs. Both men stared down at her while Artan massaged her pussy. She shuddered with the pleasure.

"Your pussy is so beautiful, Simone," Artan told her, "and you're so wet. Look at how ready you are for my brother and me."

She bit her lip. She'd been complimented by men during sex, but this went beyond what she'd experienced, and they hadn't gotten anywhere yet. With heat threatening to consume her, she watched Artan's hands and the way his eyes lit up as he stared at her. He really did think she was beautiful and seemed to be tormenting himself by not tasting her yet.

"Don't you want to lick me?" she teased. She raised her hips a little off of his brother and then settled down. Fallyn brought up a hand and squeezed her side. "Eat me, Artan."

He dropped low over her pussy and ran his tongue from one end to the other of her wet opening. She lost all strength and collapsed atop Fallyn. How the man took her full weight with no back support she didn't know, but he did it with ease.

Artan licked again and again. He laved at her like she was a dessert, and he parted her folds so he could delve his tongue deep inside of her.

She whined her pleasure. The way he sucked at her clit made her wiggle, unable to keep still. She raised her hips and tried riding his mouth, but Fallyn pushed her back down. He wanted her to rub her ass into him, but she didn't mind at all. He was so hard, she ached to have him buried inside of her from behind.

Artan continued to eat her, making hungry noises with his mouth. He moaned and he licked and gripped her thighs. He squeezed them close to his head. She had nothing to do but enjoy it. "You're going to make me come," she moaned.

"Do it," Fallyn encouraged her. "Give my brother more of your sweet come. Make her scream, Artan."

Simone was close to screaming just with that command, but Artan took it to another level when he closed his mouth over her clit and began sucking so hard it almost hurt. Her ecstasy rose to a feverish pitch. Artan's endurance was inhuman. He kept going at her, laving and then sucking at a fast pace. Her orgasm came crashing through her core, tightening muscles. Simone bit down on a scream, but Fallyn must have known it was coming. He reached around to pinch one of her nipples. The added sensation did it. She bucked and cried out. Her voice echoed over the quiet lake.

As soon as she came the first time, Artan sat up and whipped Simone into his arms. She didn't know what he was planning until she found herself back to chest with him holding her legs apart. Fallyn rolled up to a knee and buried his face between her legs. He ate up every drop of the cream she'd just released, and then he went at her clit to make her come again.

She couldn't believe their strength. The men assaulted her trembling body over and over with their tongues until she'd come half a dozen times. When it was Fallyn's turn to let her legs down so she could stand on the grass, her limbs were too weak, and she sagged. Fallyn caught her and held her close.

He lifted her chin and looked intently into her eyes. “Simone, my brother and I want more. Are you willing?”

Was he kidding? “Hell, yes.”

CHAPTER SEVEN

Simone stood in Fallyn's arms resting her head on his chest, while Artan was down on his knees behind her. She closed her eyes. She was clean, but she couldn't believe what he was doing. His tongue flicked over her ass cheek and then delved deeper. "Oh my goodness, what is he doing?"

"He is preparing to take you there. I will enter you from the front." Fallyn's formal way of speaking didn't detract from how sexy he sounded telling her they were about to double-team her.

"W-Wait," she stuttered and glanced around for her purse. "I have protection." She was sure they didn't have any. Fallyn didn't appear to know what she meant, but he released her. She found her purse and dug through it for a couple of condoms and then bit her lip. Fallyn and Artan had both opened their pants, and their cocks stood erect, thicker and longer than most any lover she'd had before. "Oh wow."

Fallyn took her exclamation for fear, and he stepped closer to take her hand. His gentleness warmed her even more. "Don't be afraid. I promise. I won't hurt you. Neither will my brother."

They were willing to do whatever she wanted, so she got them capped with little trouble. She looked around at the grass. The fact that she'd been down there in the dark was a testament to how hot they'd made her earlier. "Should we lay here?" she suggested.

Artan shook his head as he came up behind her and grasped her hips. "No, right here. We'll hold you."

Double penetration, standing up! She clutched Fallyn's shirtfront. He bent his head and kissed her lips. She tasted her essence there, and being so turned-on right now, it wasn't a bad thing.

Artan moved closer so she felt his cock head brush her ass. Fallyn dipped his knees, and she gasped when his shaft pierced her between the legs. He allowed the head to glide into her wetness but then moved back. She was still on her feet.

Simone wrapped her arms around his neck and ran the tip of her tongue over his bottom lip. His breath warmed her mouth. He was so male, so sexy. She could eat him up as much as he'd done her just a little while ago. When she pressed her breasts into his chest, he bent and grasped her legs to wind them around his waist. He didn't need to guide his cock; it slid right into her, stretching her walls and making her drop her head back in a gasp.

"Mm, yes," she murmured.

His dark gaze was locked on her as he began a slow pump. She thrilled in him watching her for some reason, knowing that she had all of his attention. He slid deeper than she thought he would, and fire he stoked licked higher until she thought she would faint.

"Fallyn," she moaned. He seemed to startle at her use of his name, and then his expression grew more intense if that was possible. He thrust harder. She cried out. Each time he ground inside of her, his pelvis rubbed her swollen clit. She bit her lip. If he didn't take it easy, she was going to come again too soon.

Before she could tumble over into bliss, he slowed his movements. She was about to protest when she realized he did it only so Artan could join them. Her second lover wet his fingers and then pushed them gently into her ass. She arched, pushing her rear into his hand. The tightness barely registered because she was so needing to come. Artan got her back entrance loose enough to fit his cock head in. He pushed in just a bit, and she fell into Fallyn's chest.

"Easy," he said in a low tone. She wasn't sure if he was speaking to her or Artan. But she was so full. One cock in her pussy, another in her ass. This was too much. She didn't think she could handle it, but then they both began to move. She whimpered. Fallyn's hold tightened. He thrust as far as he could into her and then stilled to let his brother work her from behind. "Take all of him."

"I can't," she rasped.

His lips touched her ear in a caress, but his words were a command that sent shivers up and down her spine. "Your body was made for him. Take all of Artan now."

Artan laid his head alongside hers and kissed her other ear. He turned her head so he could capture her lips in a kiss while he pumped in and out of her rear. Simone moaned against his lips, and when she was in no danger of fainting anymore, Fallyn started to move. They matched each other's rhythm while she hung sandwiched between them. Another orgasm shattered her conscious, and she cried out. Fallyn didn't stop, and neither did Artan. They worked her trembling body until she was beyond exhausted and had come so many more times that she'd lost count.

At last, they both grunted and came to their own release one behind the other. When Artan pulled out, Fallyn held her still until her breathing returned to normal. Gently, he lowered her to her feet, and then Artan took over holding her. Simone had never felt so cared for, so desired. She could still see in their eyes that they could go another few rounds, but this was new. They were both a bit rougher and definitely bigger than any lovers she'd ever had.

Artan bent to retrieve her thong, but she held onto it rather than slip into it. They discarded their used condoms into a nearby trash container.

"I guess this changes everything," Artan said with a smile.

She was about to answer, but Fallyn cut her off. "It changes nothing."

Simone frowned. "What's that supposed to mean?"

His expression was calm, not angry as before but firm as he fixed his clothes. The bastard didn't meet her eyes though when he said, "I will not make you my mate."

She didn't know why that should hurt. After all they'd done nothing but have sex, and she hadn't known them long enough for the whole mate thing. But his attitude pissed her off. "You asshole, like I don't have a say? Don't even worry about it, because I didn't intend to make you anybody special in my life either!" She turned to Artan, clearly disappointed in his twin. "I'm ready to go home. I have my cell. I'll call Blaine."

She moved away from the two of them fighting tears. Fallyn had no business ruining a perfectly good night. Blaine picked up on the second ring. "Hey, can you pick us up?"

"Be there shortly." He hung up, and she rolled her eyes. So he knew where they were. She was so over this.

Simone waited some feet away from the two men, but she could hear them arguing. When she'd gone around a tree to block them from her view, Fallyn had called out for her to stay in sight. She ignored him, but Artan had asked with more gentleness. She'd complied.

"Bastard," she grumbled low and hoped Fallyn could hear her. He looked over at her, so she figured he could. She considered whispering that his brother was better than him, but that would be childish. She just wanted to hurt him back. As it was, she fought not to cry. Men had burned her before after getting what they wanted, but she had thought she'd learned to keep them waiting until they had a firm relationship. She'd broken her rules with Artan and Fallyn and was paying for it.

On the way home, she didn't say a word to any of them, and Blaine didn't ask how it went. She tried not to think about him knowing they had sex in the frickin' woods. When they got home, she hurried up to her room, showered, and then dressed in her nightie. A knock on the door brought her up short when she was about to climb into bed. Artan and Fallyn had decided to start sleeping at Blaine's house, so she hoped it wasn't Ayana. She was in no mood to talk.

But it was Artan at the door, and she blinked in surprise. "Can I come in?" he asked.

She hesitated and looked past him. Fallyn wasn't there. Disappointment clutched her chest. She stepped back. "I guess."

They didn't say much as she clicked off the light and climbed into bed. He moved in after her and drew her into his arms. He dropped sweet kisses on her lips, and she thought he would do more, but he rested his cheek on the top of her head and held her tighter.

"Fallyn is the older of the two of us," he announced in the darkness of the room. "By ten minutes. It's not much, but he does feel the weight of carrying on our clan in the way that we have been for centuries."

Simone wrinkled her brow. "What do you mean?"

"Living closer to the animal side of us rather than the human." He brushed her cheek, and warmth spread over her. "I would leave all of that behind to stay with you. I'm only waiting for you to say the word."

She fidgeted but didn't respond.

He seemed to sense her discomfort and continued. "Fallyn is different. He thinks it weakens us to live here. He respects Reece and Blaine as well as many of the others who are able to live in both worlds, so to speak, but he thinks they're making the wrong choice."

Simone sighed. "In other words he's kind of a snob. He doesn't think my people are good enough."

Pissed off, she tried pulling away and was surprised when Artan let her go. She rolled over to face the window. The moon illuminated the room, reminding her of what they'd done under it earlier that night. She didn't regret it because it was damn good, but Fallyn didn't deserve that pleasure. If she wasn't good enough to be really with him, then she wasn't good enough to fuck either.

"Simone," Artan said.

"What."

"Come back to me. Please."

She hesitated and then rolled over to be drawn into his arms. She liked it there, and she shouldn't hold back on what Artan and she could enjoy just because of his dumb ass brother. Of course she wasn't committing to anything, but there was nothing wrong with them going out for a while. Besides, it might piss off Fallyn.

Artan kissed her for a few moments allowing his hands to roam over her body. He raised her nightie and cupped her breast. She arched into his touch and moaned when he twisted her nipple between two fingers.

"You make me hard touching you," he whispered. "I want to be inside you again, but I won't tonight."

She almost reached for him knowing if she stroked his cock, he wouldn't resist going all the way. She didn't know why she hesitated, but she felt the same in him. With supreme effort, she laid a hand over the one he still had cupping her breast. "Well then you better stop doing that. You're making me wet."

"I know." He sighed and moved his hand. "Sleep, my love. It's late."

She curled tighter into his arms and soon fell into an exhausted sleep. The next morning, when she woke up Artan wasn't there. She missed him but rose and got ready for the day without him. By the time she reached the kitchen to find some breakfast, all four men were coming in the back door. She knew the twins liked to get out in the early mornings, and Blaine and Reece often joined them.

Ayana stood at the stove scrambling eggs, and a huge plate of sausage and eggs occupied the counter beside her. Simone sighed. She didn't eat any type of pork, but Ayana uncovered another dish and she discovered turkey bacon.

"Thanks, cuz." She kissed Ayana's cheek and went to set the table. Artan caught her around the waist before she could gather silverware from the drawer and kissed her lips. She shoved at him not knowing if she was ready for all of them to know. But when she looked around from Artan's amused face, no one appeared surprised except for Ayana. *Of course.*

She set the table, head lowered and had to compete with Fallyn for space when he moved past her. His hard body cornered hers against the side of the table, and he made no real attempt to get space between them. She glared up at him. To her surprise, he dropped a kiss on her lips as well.

So he thought he could continue their sexual involvement after what he'd said last night. She rolled her eyes at him and then impulsively stretched up to her tiptoes to whisper in his ear, "Nothing happened with me and Artan last night."

His blank expression didn't change. "I know."

She squeezed the forks in her hand to keep from slapping him. *Stupid, cold-hearted jerk!*

Why the hell she wanted to appease him by telling him nothing happened, she didn't know. And for him to say he already knew made it worse. She couldn't have tormented him with thinking she was with his brother and not him if she lied. He could *smell* it.

"I want proof," she demanded in the middle of the kitchen when everyone was about to sit down to their meals. They froze at her words and stared at her.

"Uh…" Ayana began.

Simone kept standing with her hands on her hips. "You all heard me. I want proof that Artan and Fallyn are what they say they are. If it's true, then it shouldn't be a big deal. After all, Artan is claming that I'm the one for him and his brother. Fallyn denies it, but I think I have a right after…" She chewed her lip not wanting to just blurt it out in front of everyone.

No one said anything, and she grunted in frustration.

"If I get a disease because—"

"That is not possible!" Fallyn roared. She glared at him, and he seemed to make an effort to calm down. He cleared his throat "There are several advantages to what we are. You made us wear those…things, but they are not necessary."

Simone could have dropped through the floor in embarrassment. Fallyn's lips tightened. Artan stood up leaving his plate behind, and he took her hand. "We'll discuss this somewhere else so everyone else's breakfast isn't disturbed."

At first Simone hesitated. Fallyn was beyond pissed. He acted like she meant to insult them. She'd only intended to provoke them to tell her something. He had to understand her frustration. The man didn't think she was good enough for him, but his brother did. And she wanted to know what the hell made her so off-limits for marriage but good for sex. Not like she hadn't encountered men like that too.

They left the house to take their usual walk. Artan kept to her side, but Fallyn walked behind. He wasn't the type to follow anyone, but she figured he wanted to keep them in sight.

"Tell me about why Fallyn said it's impossible for me to catch anything from you," she asked Artan. "Is it because he knows he's clean?"

Artan nodded. "That and we have no known illness or disease that can stay in our body for more than a few hours. We have a natural ability to heal, inside and out."

Her eyes grew round. "So if you were shot, you'd heal right up within an hour?"

"Yes, but of course it's possible that if I was shot in the heart, I might bleed to death. If my head's cut off…"

She cringed and swallowed. "I get it. Thanks. So, in other words, no disease could last long enough in your body to be passed on to anyone else."

"Right. And that is a common feature for all of us," he explained.

Simone glanced over her shoulder at Fallyn. His angry eyes met hers, but he didn't say anything. The man had no right to be pissed off, but she ignored him and turned back to Artan. She moved closer to him and took his arm. Artan, recognizing that she wanted to whisper in his ear, bent closer to her as they strolled down the block. "I get how he likes to keep things as it was in the dark ages with your clan, but why am *I* not good. It can't be race—or can it?"

Artan stopped and studied her face. She fidgeted under his stare. But then he tugged her into his arms to hug her. She gave his chest a push without results. He lifted her chin and kissed her lips before nuzzling her neck. "His rejection bothers you, doesn't it? You don't want to admit you feel something for him."

"I feel irritation toward him."

He grinned. "It's not your race. Or I should say, it's not because you're human." He broke off and peered over at his brother. Fallyn was standing leaning against a tree with his arms folded over his chest. The inquiring expression on his face let Simone know in a heartbeat that Fallyn heard every word they'd spoken. That alone told her the man wasn't natural. He couldn't be.

Artan cast his gaze up toward the sky as he thought. After some time, he looked back at Simone. "What is it I heard someone say at that party the other night? Oh, it's because you are a 'city girl.'" Simone's jaw dropped even though she could have guessed the full reason. He went on. "You were disgusted with the thought of lying in the grass at night because of bugs. There have been times when Fallyn and I have not seem humans or spoken the human language for months because we are out there among nature, sleeping in caves sometimes."

She stared. "Are you serious?"

He nodded. "We smelled it before you arrived at Ayana's, or it could be said that we sensed it. I'm not sure. We both knew you were our mate, but Fallyn decided right away that you weren't right for him."

"Because of coming from the city," she snapped. She focused on Fallyn. "Who needs him? Why are you even still here, Fallyn? No one's holding you back from returning to your cave." She knew she was talking from hurt feelings, and she wanted to hurt him back. To her surprise, he did seem bothered, but the glimpse of it disappeared as fast as it had shown up.

Artan took her hand. "Come with me."

They continued down the block and then took a different direction from the ones they'd taken previously. Soon they came upon a small park with a tiny man-made pond. Ducks relaxed on the surface of the water, and a narrow path led around the edge of the water. Artan guided her along it to the far side of the park in an area more dense with trees. When he glanced around and began removing his clothes, she smirked.

"Are you going to flash me now, Artan, or you want to have sex again to prove your animal makeup."

He winked. "Sex yes, but not now. I think I proved myself last night."

She let her gaze rake over his sexy, hard body. Just flirting like they were doing had his big cock standing at attention. "That you did, boyfriend. That you did."

Simone's next words died on her lips as Artan's body began to change. He grew bigger, and hair sprouted on his body, even his face. She stumbled back and almost fell, but Fallyn was there in an instant to catch her. Not sure if she should shake him off, because whatever was happening to Artan he could do too, or whether she should jump into his arms for safety, she stood frozen in place. Artan's bones snapped and popped. He growled like a man one second and then as a beast the next. His teeth grew sharp and pointed. Where his fingernails were clear showing pink underneath as a man, they transformed to long curved claws that were as black as midnight.

Simone didn't know she was shaking until Fallyn's arms tightened at her waist. He stroked her belly and whispered comforting words in her ear. "It's okay, my love. Don't be afraid. Artan would never hurt you."

If she weren't so scared, she'd wonder at how gentle he was being, how he'd called her "my love" just like Artan had before. But she couldn't do anything other than stare at Artan. Her eyes hurt they were so wide.

He'd gone from a man to a full-grown black bear in less than a minute, and he had to be a good one thousand pounds. In that form, if he jumped on her, he'd crush her.

He raised his head and aimed black eyes at her. She squeaked in fear. The bear took a step in her direction. Simone screamed. Fallyn put a hand over her mouth. "Stay where you are, idiot. She is afraid."

Artan stopped cold, and she could have sworn she saw sadness in his eyes that he terrified her. The bear hunkered down to the ground, and then as quickly as he'd changed, he was in human form slipping into his clothes. He left his shoes off and rushed over to her. Simone pressed herself back against Fallyn's chest, but Artan wouldn't let her remain afraid. He gathered her into his arms and kissed her lips, her eyes, her hair. "Don't be scared, please, Simone. I wouldn't hurt you. I'm fully aware of who and what I am in that state. And even if I wasn't, it's impossible to hurt my mate. Do you understand?"

He made her look at him. His expression was so tender, she felt herself melting. But that didn't mean she accepted this. "So all of you can do that?" she whispered.

"Yes, except Reece is a brown bear."

"I believe you now." She put a hand over her eyes and then rubbed her temple. "It doesn't mean…I just can't wrap my head around…How can this kind of thing exist?"

"Easy," Fallyn told her, still standing close behind. Why was he still here, she wondered. He could just go and leave Artan. They were close, and it was obvious Fallyn was the more dominant of the two, but he didn't appear to be overprotective of him. Why did he even come to the city if he hated it so much?

She turned a little in Artan's arms to look at Fallyn. His gaze was riveted to her face as if he didn't want to look away in case she zapped out. But then she began to think it was more than that. He put his hand up and stroked her face. She wanted to resist him, but instead, she turned her face into his palm. Somehow she drifted out of Artan's arms and into Fallyn's. He lowered his head and kissed her deeply. His tongue parted her lips to glide inside her mouth. Simone moaned and arched into his hold. The man shouldn't be given the time of day, but she was already weak to him—weaker than she'd been with anyone other than Artan.

Fallyn clutched her around her shoulders and ran his other hand down her back to her ass. He squeezed her cheek, and she felt his cock grow hard between them. When his fingers pushed against her shorts seeking her back entrance, she shook with desire. He released her mouth and looked down as he breathed in deep. Now she knew they weren't crazy. Fallyn took her scent in through his nose as if she was a drug and it was getting him high. Maybe that's why he hadn't left yet. Once again, she wondered if it was the same with them for any woman who was hot and horny.

"I want to fuck you right here and now," he said in a gruff tone.

Simone scanned the area. There were some people over toward the beginning of the park. "It's risky," she commented. "I'm wondering if we'll ever do it in a bed like normal people."

"We're not normal." His eyes blazed at her, and she didn't resist when he led her behind a tree that was only as wide as he was. They were hidden from view, but if she opened her legs to wrap around him, no one would wonder what they were doing. Fallyn had the solution to that. He pinched her shorts' button open and lowered her zipper. "I am going to lift you up and put you on my cock. Keep your legs together. It will be a tight squeeze, but you will like it."

Her shorts and panties slid down her legs. Artan caught them to keep them from touching the ground, and he helped her step out of them. She shivered. If anyone came from the other direction, her ass would be on display for them to see. Artan stood behind them, and Fallyn pushed her back just enough for him to crouch in front of her. When he buried his head between her legs, she gasped and chewed her bottom lip. What she wanted to do was scream her pleasure, but she couldn't repeat what happened by the lake. Half the county must have heard her then.

She laid one hand on the tree to brace herself and the other on the back of Fallyn's head. She watched as he ate her out. His tongue slithered over her pussy, scooping up her come. He parted her folds to push in deeper, and she keened. "Fallyn," she whimpered.

He growled hearing her call his name and gave one final suck before he stood up again. The man wasted no time hoisting her into the air and bringing her down on his cock. He wasn't gentle, but he didn't need to be. His roughness set her on fire. She wanted to shout his name all over Charlotte, but she clamped down on it. Fallyn pounded his big dick inside her until her head spun. Her orgasm when it came took her by surprise. Powerful muscle contractions had her shaking and limp in his arms.

Fallyn continued to thrust into her. He squeezed her ass as he pushed upward. His teeth were clenched, and he didn't take his eyes off her once. Another low growl rent the quiet around them, and then she felt it. His warm come filled her pussy with Fallyn sighing behind it.

Watching them must have gotten Artan excited. The two men switched places, flipping her from one man's arms to the next as if she weighed nothing. In a heartbeat, Fallyn's cock left her only to be replaced by Artan's. His movements were unhurried and gentle. He took her slow and whispered naughty but sweet things in her ear. She melted against him, wrapping her arms around his neck.

When she murmured his name, he too was affected. He shivered, and his eyes went dark like when he was about to change. A hint of fear snaked up her system, but she didn't pull away. Another orgasm began to build, and she dropped her head back, eyes closed. She felt rather than saw Fallyn move up behind. He smacked her ass and then stroked the sting away. *Spanking!*

She came hard, but Artan didn't let her go. His pace increased, and Fallyn brought his stiff palm up again on her cheek. She whimpered.

"Do you want me to stop, Simone?" he asked in a harsh tone.

"No, never," she moaned.

He did it again. By now they must have called attention with all the noise, but she didn't care. Fallyn spanking her and Artan pumping his amazing dick into her snatch was driving her insane. She wished she could encircle his waist with her legs, but Fallyn hadn't let her lift them. Just like his brother, Artan was a tight squeeze in, but that made it all the hotter. She cried out their names one after another, and then she came at the same time as Artan.

She must have fainted at the sheer bliss of the experience, because the next time she opened her eyes, she was sitting on Fallyn's lap on the grass. Artan had tissues in his hands tossing them in a trashcan. She wondered where he'd gotten them.

"You are fine?" Fallyn asked. Something thrilled inside of her at his formal way of speaking. She'd miss him when he was gone. And because it upset her so much, she decided not to think about it.

"Yeah, I'm good." She stood up and was glad that they'd thought to put her clothes back on. Man, talk about good sex anytime she'd blacked out from it. "We should get back. I have to work this afternoon, and I need a shower."

"Of course." Artan came over and held his hand out. She took it, and they walked together with Fallyn behind them along the path. When they got close to the couple at the other side of the small park, the man let out a low whistle. Simone blushed. So they weren't as secretive about it as they thought. She peeked at the woman and found her face was flaming red. Simone laughed. At least the woman was more embarrassed. She didn't regret it. Having Fallyn and Artan together was fun. Call her a slut. She didn't give a damn.

CHAPTER EIGHT

Simone left the restaurant early for a change. The sun hadn't gone down yet, and that was always nice. She felt like the day had passed her by when she had to wait until eleven to get off. Still, her feet hurt, and she was tired. All day, the customers were in a mood or she just wasn't feeling it. They were rude. She had trouble keeping snide remarks to herself, and her boss wasn't happy. The only reason he hadn't fired her ass, he told her, was because he needed the help. She of course apologized and promised she would get it together by tomorrow night.

When she got outside, she found only Artan waiting for her, and he seemed subdued. She frowned. "What is Fallyn in a pissy mood again? Well join the club. I'm not feeling too happy either!"

Artan didn't answer, so she stopped walking. He put his hand in hers and pulled her along. "Come on. We'll miss the bus." Blaine had offered to pick her up and take her to work, but she hated depending on anyone. She'd take the offer if the weather was bad, but on a normal basis, no way. And soon enough, she'd get her own place. The only reason she'd delayed was because Blaine had asked her to wait a little while. He knew Artan and Fallyn would follow her, and he didn't think they were ready to be loose in the city. He was more nursemaid to them as far as she was concerned. After all, the two of them walked down to her job all the time to pick her up and ride the bus back with her. Fallyn hated it, but he'd always come. Tonight was different.

"Is he mad at me for some reason?" she pressed.

"No."

She stopped walking and stomped her foot. "Look, you tell me what's going on, Artan, or I'm going to take so long we miss the bus, and you'll have to carry me all the way home."

He chuckled low but then sobered right away. "That's no problem at all. If you prefer, I will be glad to do it." He moved like he was going to lift her up, and she shoved at him.

"You would, wouldn't you?" She shook her head. "Crazy man." They fell into step again. "Tell me, Artan. I can see something's bothering you. I like seeing your smiling face. If you're down, the world is coming to an end because you're always happy."

He sighed. "We have a visitor from our home. We didn't expect her."

Her. Simone chewed her lip. So this person, whoever she was, had caused Fallyn not to come with Artan to pick her up. And she'd made the always upbeat Artan down in the dumps. Who the hell was she? Where Simone had been all ready to drag the truth out of Artan before, now she hesitated. Since she'd come from the same place as they had and Artan was being kind of mysterious, it was obvious that she was one of them.

As Simone climbed on the bus and found her seat, she brought to mind how Artan had looked in bear form. He'd been completely animal from what she could see. Nothing had indicated that he could be a person anytime he felt like it. So this woman could do the same? And why had she come? Was she another cousin or something else?

All these thoughts swirled through her head as they neared home, but neither she nor Artan spoke a word. They got off the bus and walked the block down to Lawnwood Drive. On Ayana's street, Simone glanced over to Artan to find him rolling his shoulders and neck as if to ease the tension in them. From the tight expression, she didn't think it worked.

When they drew up to the driveway, Artan moved closer to her and took her hand. She looked up at him, but he appeared closed off. She scanned the neighborhood. A couple of neighbors working on their front lawns waved. She returned the greeting, but turned back to the house. Before they got halfway up the drive, Blaine's front door opened. A woman appeared, and stepped out. Artan pulled Simone to a stop.

Simone's mouth went dry at seeing Fallyn appear behind the woman. She focused on the beauty—because that word described her with an understatement. Her hair was thick and vibrant, blonde, stretching all the way down to her waist. She had big light eyes. Simone figured they were probably blue or green, but she couldn't tell from the short distance. Either way, they were framed with thick, curved lashes. Her nose was pert, and her mouth a perfect pouting bow. If she were a size two, Simone would be surprised, but even that little, she had curves and decent-size boobs that hadn't succumbed to gravity in the least.

As small as she was and as fully feminine, there was a danger about her as well. The woman took a step in Simone's direction, and Ayana's entire household along with Artan and Fallyn moved between the two of them. Simone looked at them all like they were crazy. She hadn't even heard the door open at her cousin's house.

"I have a right," the woman was saying somewhere beyond the big male bodies blocking Simone's view.

She shook her head. "Hold up. Y'all out here 'cause she feels like starting something with me?" Simone pushed through Reece and Blaine, but Artan wouldn't let her get past his shoulder. At least she could see now. Ms. Thing's *blue* eyes were trained on her with such fire and hatred, if Simone didn't stand firm, the heat of it would have made her stumble back. "Bitch, anytime you feeling froggy we can go."

She sprang at Simone, but Fallyn caught her around the waist and tugged her to him. Simone flinched with jealousy she hoped no one had noticed.

"Stop, Katrina," Fallyn told her. "You cannot attack her. Artan has claimed her as his mate."

"But that wasn't good enough for her," Katrina spat, still glaring at

Fallyn. "I smell her on you."

"And why should that bother you?" Simone demanded.

No one answered. She thought Katrina would, but Fallyn was busy dragging her back to Blaine's house.

"Let's take this inside," Reece suggested. "We don't need the neighborhood in on family business."

Ayana came over and wrapped an arm around Simone's shoulders to guide her toward the house. Simone gave in and went. "She's staying over there with Artan and Fallyn?" she asked her cousin. Ayana didn't meet her eyes. "You know what's going on, Ayana. What's this all about?"

"Shifter stuff," was all Ayana admitted.

Rather than sit in the living room and be ignored, Simone went up to her room to shower and change. When she took her time about coming back, someone knocked at her door. "Come in," she called.

Ayana opened the door. "Sweetie, can you come down? Artan and Fallyn want to talk to you."

"They couldn't come themselves?"

She frowned. "We don't want to provoke anything. She—"

"Needs us to walk on eggshells?" Simone crossed her arms over her chest and stayed right where she was. The truth was, she wanted to get to the bottom of things, but she was feeling a little emotional. Maybe it was the fact that her time of the month was near and she was PMSing. If she went down there and got to crying for no reason, she'd never forgive herself. By that same token, she could just as easily fly off the handle in anger like what had almost happened outside.

Ayana slipped into the room and shut the door quietly. "Look, from what I can gather from Reece," she whispered, "they do things way differently where the twins come from. Katrina feels like Fallyn all but accepted her as his mate, and when another woman comes into the picture who has not been declared his mate, Katrina has the right to kill her."

"Whoa! What?" Simone almost shouted.

"Shh!" Ayana listened at the door. "You know their damn hearing is good. Sweetie, I want you safe. That woman looks nuts, and if you haven't figured it out yet, she's a shifter. She can frickin' turn into a bear just like them. She's not like one of those hootchies we came across in New York. If that was the case, I'd say kick her ass and get it over with."

Simone flopped down on her bed and shut her eyes. "I get it. She'd turn me into filet mignon in a heartbeat. It's not like I asked them to pay me attention. They came after me."

"I know." Ayana spread her hands. "I see the same possessiveness in them that's in Reece and Blaine. They knew right from the start that you're meant for them. But it's like this thing with Fallyn and Artan is different. Reece told me he's never seen one of them deny their mate. The whole conflict comes in when that mate is human. For Fallyn to rej—um…"

"You can say it." Simone waved her hand like it didn't matter. And it shouldn't really. She'd known them only a short time. But it did matter. "He rejected me. I don't blame him, because if he thinks I'm living out in the bushes, he's crazy. Same goes for Artan."

"You have to see it. It's not the bushes." Ayana laughed. "Yeah, it's exclusive, and no one comes out there unless they belong, but it's not the dark ages with like no electricity or something."

"Like you said, things are different where Artan and Fallyn come from," Simone quipped. She stood up. "Well, I'm not one to run from anything, even a losing battle, so I'm going down there."

Ayana nodded. "I'm with you, and I'll back you up with whatever you decide. If you want the twins to leave, just say so, and I'll get Blaine to get rid of them."

Simone opened her bedroom door and started out. "Somehow I don't think he'd have a say in what they do when it comes to me." Her words were more resigned than self-assured. Soon she'd know one way or another what waited for her downstairs.

When she went into the living room, Simone found the four men but no Katrina. That was a relief at least. Ayana moved up from behind her. "Reece and Blaine, can you help me with the grilling out back? Simone." She touched Simone's arms, her eyes saying call her if she needed her.

Simone nodded and then turned to consider where to sit. Both men's eyes were trained on her. Artan touched the seat beside him, and Fallyn stood frozen by the window looking like a caged animal. She ignored him and went over to sit beside Artan. He reached between her legs and cupped her inner thigh. Not so high she would get hot, but intimate enough to stake his claim.

Not one to beat around the bush, she said, "So is she going to try to kill me or what?"

Artan's eyes turned dark, and he growled. "Over my dead body."

Fallyn frowned. "She understands you haven't made a claim on me. She won't try anything."

Simone told herself not to ask, but the words tumbled out of her mouth anyway. "She considers herself your mate, right? And she has no reason to think otherwise. You were basically up here cheating with me while she was waiting at home."

His eyes matched Artan's. "I was not cheating. You don't understand."

"I guess I don't. Whatever. You can do whatever you want to do. Just keep your grizzly out of my face. Woman to woman I'd wipe the floor with her."

For a moment, she thought she saw a flash of pride in Fallyn's face, but then it was gone. He had no idea she was fronting. In reality, Katrina scared her, but she wasn't going to let that show to anyone. It annoyed her that she couldn't tell what Fallyn was truly like. They'd spoken a little, but not enough to feel like she knew him, which probably meant she shouldn't be sleeping with him either. But the man was hot as hell. Up until now, she would never have thought he would leave a woman at home and have sex with another. Simone considered herself a good judge of character and always believed a dog would show his true colors after while. Maybe this was that time.

Artan squeezed her thigh to gain her attention. Simone glanced up at him. "I was thinking," he said, "I would like you to come out to our homestead to get a better feel for how we live."

Simone blinked at him. "To a cave?"

He grinned. She thought she heard a grunt from Fallyn, but when she looked over there, he was staring out the window, face blank.

"No, not a cave," Artan told her. "We have property with a few small houses on it. Similar to this, but with much more grounds between and lots more trees around. Only the road in is paved."

"Lovely," she mumbled. Faced with the thought of giving Artan up without getting to know him better, she decided to give it a try. She wasn't *all* manicured nails and weaves. "Yeah, sure. That sounds like fun."

While he discussed a few things with his brother, she wondered if she could actually do it. They were so different from her, so obviously in love with the outdoors while she feared anything to do with it. Here she was sitting there considering whether all her hair products, lotions, and creams could be taken along. If she took that stuff and wore it, it was likely the bugs would eat her alive.

She thought about how Katrina looked when she'd seen her. If the woman wore makeup, it was so natural, it wasn't visible. But then with those lashes, she didn't need a thing on her eyes. Simone put a finger up to bite her nail. Artan slipped his hand behind hers and threaded his fingers with hers.

"Come on. Let's eat. I'm starved." He stood up and took her with him. Something inside wanted to reach out and take Fallyn's hand too, but she forced herself not to turn around as she followed Artan out back.

Reece had the grill going, and he was taking steaks off of it. Blaine was setting chairs around the picnic table they'd opted for rather than the smaller round one with the umbrella. With big men of her own and with

Fallyn, Artan, and Simone, they needed more space. But even that was intimate because the shifters were built like linebackers.

Simone left Artan's side to go help Ayana toss a salad and set the table. While her cousin chatted like there was no tension in the air, Simone half-listened. Her attention was on Artan and his brother, so when Fallyn's low comments to something Blaine said cut off dead, she turned to see what was the matter. Katrina stood at the side of the house watching in silence. Her unreadable gaze slid from Fallyn to Simone and back again.

No one moved, and then Ayana went forward to take her hand. "Welcome, Katrina. We're just about to have dinner. You can join us if you like."

Artan's hand settled on Simone's lower back. She hadn't seen him move from where Blaine and Fallyn were standing. She liked the comfort his touch brought, but she stared at Fallyn not meaning too. He looked back at her and then drifted toward the table to sit down.

"Thank you. I'd love to," Katrina said at last. Some of the mounting tension eased, but not much. She walked over to Fallyn's side and took a place beside him. *Princess used to being served, I guess.*

Simone finished mixing the salad and brought it over to the picnic table. She set plates in front of the men, and Katrina snatched away the one she was about to put before Fallyn. They glared at each other. Katrina rose.

"Sit down," Fallyn snapped, and to Simone's surprise, she obeyed.

Simone considered skipping giving her a plate but decided she wasn't going to sink to the witch's level, and she tossed one in front of the woman. Katrina looked like she wanted to pick pieces of Simone from her teeth. Simone swept Katrina from head to toe and dismissed her with a shift of her eyes.

She took a seat next to Artan, and when everyone was settled, Ayana said the blessing, and they dug in. Simone was somewhat annoyed that Ayana was playing the peacemaker, but she should be grateful. Her attitude and Fallyn's commands were probably the only things keeping Katrina at bay.

"So, Katrina," Ayana began, "have you known Fallyn and Artan long?"

Katrina ate with as much gusto as the men—the first unlovely thing about her. "Of course. We grew up together. It was always understood that I would be Fallyn's mate. In fact, his mother approved of the match." Her gaze shifted to Simone, the light of triumph obvious. "Before she passed."

Simone squeezed Artan's hand under the table. They had discussed his mother's dying briefly before but not in any great detail. His father had remarried. The two of them had had Artan and Fallyn late in life, and they were considered miracles.

"So what are y'all like kissing cousins or something?" Simone asked. She directed the question to Artan.

He smiled at her and brought her hand to his lips to kiss. A tingle of awareness shot through her body, and she felt his muscles shift in the leg that touched hers. Fallyn's fork clanked on his plate, drawing a few eyes to him. Simone squirmed. Was she excited enough for him to pick up the scent? She hadn't thought so, but she could feel the burning hatred radiating off of Katrina's stare.

"No," Artan told her. "Katrina's family has the same problems with growth that ours does, and many years ago, we decided to share the same lands and mate across families if possible."

Another point for her, Simone thought. Artan's words only proved her claim on Fallyn. Something tightened in her chest. She didn't realize she'd closed her eyes and wasn't moving until Artan leaned over to press his lips to her ear.

"Eat your food, Simone." His command made her jump. Not because it was mean, but because he sounded exactly like Fallyn. If she didn't know any better, she would have thought he was channeling his twin. When she picked up her fork and looked across the table, she found Fallyn's eyes on her. They were never far, even with Katrina clinging to his arm and trying to dominate his attention. If Simone knew nothing else, she knew that Fallyn was having trouble dismissing her from his thoughts and desires. But how far would he go to wash her away?

Simone was not one to let Katrina dominate the conversation to prove she had a stronger claim on Fallyn, so she jumped in and turned it to other topics. To her satisfaction and Katrina's annoyance, everyone at the table joined in. Soon dinner was finished, and everyone helped to clean up.

Before they were done, Katrina strolled toward the side of the house with hips swinging unnecessarily hard. The grace she moved with in the miniskirt she wore was more like a sleek jungle cat than a lumbering bear. One of the amazing things Simone had noticed about the shifters was that their eyes never strayed from their mate, which was awesome. She'd known too many men with wandering eyes that they couldn't control in the presence of a beautiful woman. Even with their girlfriend standing next to them, their gazes would dart back and forth to a deep cleavage or big butt. Reece, Blaine, and Artan didn't turn their heads in Katrina's direction, nor did they seem tempted to. Fallyn did, and that got to Simone. However, his next words made her wonder if it was more than about watching Katrina's ass.

"Katrina, you did not help clean up or offer thanks for the meal," he chastised.

She paused and turned back. Her eyebrows rose at the irritation in his tone, but then she pouted. "I thought you and I could get some alone time next door. You're coming, aren't you?"

What the "alone time" would entail was more than clear. Princess didn't give a damn about anyone but herself and getting her hooks into Fallyn.

Fallyn didn't move or say a word, but it was obvious he was pissed at her attitude. The feeling got through to Katrina, and she offered Ayana an impatient thanks. Fallyn offered his, helped to finish cleaning up, and then disappeared with Katrina. Simone wrestled trash bags with more vehemence than necessary, and then Artan took them from her hands.

He leaned in and kissed her before whispering in her ear. "He's so attentive to her to keep her calm. He doesn't want her to hurt you, and of course he wants to keep the peace in this place that's not used to how we settle things."

Simone waved her hand. "Whatever. Like I gave a crap."

She went to her room and flipped through a few magazines before calling it a night. By one in the morning, she was staring at the ceiling, unable to stop wondering what was happening next door in Blaine's house. Never—*ever*—did she give a man the time of day if there was even a hint of another woman. She knew what it could do to self-esteem. Hell, she had her mother for an example of what a woman would stoop to if she put up with a man's mess too long. Simone would have resorted to her old standbys and showed the ass what a great time she was having without him. But she couldn't do that with Artan. Fallyn wasn't jealous of Artan being with her.

Sighing in frustration, she rolled over to her side. When a voice reached her from the street, she got up on her knees and glanced out the window. Her bedroom overlooked the front of the house, and she was surprised to see the twins standing side by side barefoot. Fallyn wore jeans and nothing else, and Artan wore just a pair of shorts. Desire curled in her belly, and on cue, both men turned to look up at her window.

She smothered a laugh and opened the window. "Artan, come up?"

He didn't hesitate. She ran downstairs to the first floor to let him in, and he raised her into his arms. Over his shoulder, she caught site of Fallyn's face. Although he kept it neutral, she didn't miss the stiff way he stood, the clenching of his fists at his sides, and his lips compressed.

Artan kicked the door closed and carried her upstairs to her room. Simone settled where he laid her on the bed, and she held up her arms.

Artan weighted down the bed with a knee and then lay just where she wanted him.

CHAPTER NINE

They arrived at Artan and Fallyn's homestead a little after four the next day. Simone had arranged for emergency time off from work, and Ayana who worked from home with her good friend had no trouble getting the time. All the men seemed to come and go as they pleased. Simone thought it must be nice since she wondered if she'd actually have a job when she returned.

Just as Artan had described there were trees everywhere, and the road leading into the area was the only one that was paved. Still, the community was nice, and it could have passed for a suburb farther out in the country. Simone had expected to see random bears wandering about, and her stomach had stayed in knots thinking that. But Artan had assured her that they would all pick up her and Ayana's human scents long before they arrived and wouldn't want to scare them. So no one would appear in shifted form. She breathed a sigh of relief to find he was right.

At the end of the narrow lane, Blaine stopped his truck in front of one of the larger houses. Simone and Artan had been the only two to ride out here with them, while the others rode with Reece in his SUV. Artan stepped out of the truck and held out his hand to Simone. She took it and followed him to the dirt road.

The door to the house opened, and a big man stood in the doorway in overalls and no shirt. *Okay, country. Nice.* She suppressed a giggle, and Artan's handsome face mirrored her humor. Aside from the attire, one couldn't mistake that this was Artan and Fallyn's father. As big as he was, she couldn't imagine he grew much when he transformed.

"Dad," Artan said, "this is my mate, Simone."

She quirked an eyebrow at Artan. He was jumping the gun. She knew how he thought of her, but she'd only conceded to them being lovers. Nothing more.

To her surprise and slight disgust, Artan's father's gaze slid from her face to her cleavage and stayed there. "Hello, beautiful. You can call me Carl."

He took Simone up into a literal bear hug that Artan had to extricate her from before there was damage—or sexual assault.

"Nice to meet you," she said in a dry tone. She stepped slightly behind Artan's protective shoulder, and his father laughed like it was all a joke. *Yeah right. Old perv.*

A younger woman who appeared to be around Simone and Ayana's age came out. She was poured into denim shorts and a tube top that looked like it was ready to snap under the pressure of her massive fake boobs. She wore too much makeup, her hair was teased too high, and if the sun glinted off the rock on her finger, they'd all be blinded. Human, Simone thought. She prayed this wasn't another possible mate for one of the twins, but then it registered that a thin wedding band accompanied the diamond ring.

Simone watched the woman curl on Carl's arm. She couldn't be. Ayana drew up next to Simone looking at the woman too. They glanced at each other, and her cousin's thoughts matched hers if the expression on her face was anything to go by. *Gold digger.* Artan and Fallyn's father had to be pushing seventy if not there.

"This is my wife, Tammy," Carl told her. "Say hello, Tammy." He said the words as if he had to explain everything to her, but Simone caught the look in the woman's eyes. She was no idiot.

"Hey, y'all, welcome," she said between popping gum. This woman did not live in caves, that was for sure. Her big overly made up eyes assessed Ayana and Simone, and she didn't like what she saw. Judged them as competition, Simone guessed. But she didn't have to worry. Simone had never taken an old man as a lover, and she damn sure wasn't starting now.

Fallyn drew up. Simone wondered what was the accusatory look he tossed his brother. "Father."

"Welcome back, Fallyn. I see Katrina found you." His father's response was cool but not as cold as Fallyn's greeting. There was clear dislike.

Fallyn ignored the man's second response and spared his stepmother a glance. "Tammy."

After all the greetings were done, they were invited into the house. Simone discovered it was Carl's house, and the twins had a separate place of their own not far away. With all the hostility between Fallyn and his father, she didn't blame them. And Simone would have killed if she personally had to live with his stepmother.

Carl dismissed his wife to go do something with herself, and he was the one to show Ayana and her men to a room. "You," he told Simone, standing too close, "can come this way. I have a room right—"

"No." Fallyn's voice, although it didn't rise above his father's, was still powerful enough to shut the older man up. "She will not stay here."

Katrina butted in. Simone had wondered where her little hot tail lived and hoped it wasn't in Fallyn's house. "That's not really for you to say, is it, honey?" The endearment held none of the affection. She was just pissed that Fallyn defended Simone.

"Simone's staying with me," Artan told his father. He tugged her out of reach of his father, and Simone looked up at the big man to note the disappointment. What the heck went on out here that he thought he could just put Simone in some room where he'd have easy access to her? As she followed Artan back down the hall and out of the house, she shivered.

Later, after she was settled, they returned to the big house for dinner.

One of the women in the clan had cooked because Tammy didn't know her way around the kitchen. Ayana and Simone had offered to help but were refused, so they sat down to enjoy the feast. Simone quit eating after she thought she'd gained about five pounds at the dinner table alone and stepped outside when no one was looking.

Too many people were around in Carl's house, and she was glad she wasn't staying there. Artan and Fallyn had said they had a small clan, and she guessed they did, but all of them were close by. She felt restricted in the house with people dropping over constantly. No wonder a large dinner had been prepared because there had been at least twenty at the table.

Outside the sun had gone down, and Simone sat on the banister of the porch. A cool breeze stirred her hair, and she imagined she heard the sounds of traffic in the distance rather than the whistles of crickets or the spin of cicadas. If she had any sense, she would stay indoors until it was time to go back to Artan's house. But she was trying to accept nature as it was. The task was not easy.

A swish of the bushes nearby made her jump, and she was about to hightail it back inside when Fallyn came into view. She'd never seen him leave the house. He met her startled gaze and rested his hands on the banister beside her. With an impressive display of muscle, he hoisted himself up by his palms and leaped over the railing. She would have openly admired the view but didn't want him to know how he affected her.

He settled beside her, leaning on the railing with hands folded in front of him. "I am surprised to see you out here. I thought you would be afraid."

"I am." She saw no reason to lie.

He raised a hand as if to touch her cheek, thought better of it, and then dropped his hand. A second later, he followed through and ran the back of his hand over her cheek. Simone kept expecting someone to interrupt them, but no one did. Fallyn moved closer to her until his lips brushed hers. She had to think of something fast to distract herself before she jumped him and begged him to take her right there.

"It seems like you don't like your father," she said.

That got him. He paused in his movements and looked down at her. For a moment, she thought he was going to kiss her again, but he said. "No, I do not. I respect him because he is my father, but no, I do not like him." Fallyn's lips tightened, and he looked off into the darkness. "My mother lay dying a few years ago, and he was busy with *her*. I cannot blame her exactly, not fully. He was always too attentive to women who were not his own. If one of us finds that more than one other is his mate, that is fine. But my father liked to take other people's mates. While we blame my mother's death on old age—because they did have Artan and I late in their years, and she was older than my father—I believe a part of it was a loss of will to stay in this life."

Simone laid her hand on his forearm. "Oh man, I am so sorry, Fallyn. That must really hurt, and I can't imagine. My mother gets on my last nerve, but she's still around at least."

He laid his hand over hers and squeezed. Simone dipped her head and rested it on his shoulder. For a long while, they didn't move. The breeze stirred between them, flipping a few strands of Simone's hair onto her face. Fallyn gently brushed them away and caressed her cheek. She couldn't believe she was out here feeling okay. The slight panic she'd experienced earlier before he came out had subsided, and she remembered how it was like no big deal at the lake that time they first had sex. With Artan or Fallyn, nature wasn't so bad.

He ran his hand down her back, stopping just above her ass. She moved closer. She knew she shouldn't, but just like Fallyn was having a hard time letting go of his desire for her, she was too. Maybe it was because she saw his desire and his longing behind his cold eyes, or it could be a flaw in her character just like his stepmother. She wanted it all. She wanted both Artan and Fallyn, and that just seemed greedy.

He raised her chin, and his hand was so large it engulfed her neck where it lay. She felt vulnerable to him. His strength, she bet, was such that he could snap her like a twig. But she wasn't afraid of him. Fallyn's warm breath heated her lips. He stared at them, temptation plain in his gaze. "You fucked him last night."

The words were spoken so low, she couldn't be sure if it was an accusation. She also couldn't remember if he'd ever used such harsh words before. "You had Katrina to warm your bed."

Once she'd said it, she wished she could take it back. She'd revealed how jealous she was, and she never liked a man to have that much power over her. Fallyn kissed her hard and cruel, and she melted into his arms. He reached between them and snapped the buttons on her blouse. She gasped at hearing them ping on the floor and then at the feel of him squeezing her breast.

Fallyn abused her little nipple, twisting and tugging at it until she was ready to come with that feeling and nothing else. He punished her, and he didn't have a right to. She tried willing herself to pull away but only managed to end their kiss. She couldn't pull herself out of his arms. When she opened her eyes, Fallyn was looking past her. He gave a small shake of his head, and she tried looking, but he held her still.

"Who was that?" she demanded.

"No one," he said. "Come on. I'll walk you back to our house. I assume you don't want to go inside?"

"No." They walked in silence for a while. She frowned. "It was Artan, wasn't it? Y'all always know when I'm excited."

"Yes."

She waited for him to elaborate, but he didn't. "If you think we're having sex, you're sadly mistaken. I'm not anyone's other woman. You made it plain how you really feel about me, and you already have Katrina."

He frowned. "Simone…"

Speak of the devil, she stepped out from between two houses. "There you are, Fallyn." Hadn't anyone ever told her a woman doesn't chase a man? She lets him chase her. Simone shook her head. From the looks of it, Katrina was going to catch Fallyn by any means necessary.

When the blonde's countenance turned stormy, Simone had a good idea she knew they had kissed, and just to piss her off Simone ran her tongue over her lips as if to taste Fallyn again.

Katrina started forward, but Fallyn stopped her, calling out her name. Just the sight of him holding Katrina was more than Simone was willing to stand there and put up with. "I can find my own way back," she snapped. "You have your hands full."

Before he could utter another word, she hurried off almost skipping down the lane. When she got to Artan and Fallyn's home, she stomped through the door and slammed it behind her. She didn't care whether they heard it back where they stood in the road or not. She wasn't playing the game Fallyn was playing. She wanted out.

Simone walked down the short hall to her room and went in to prepare for bed. By the time she had cleaned up and changed into her nightie, thoughts of Artan and Fallyn filled her mind. The house was small but seemed gargantuan all alone in it. Especially when she couldn't get the twins out of her head. She came to the top she'd taken off earlier and remembered the buttons. For the life of her, she couldn't remember whether it had hung open showing off her breasts in front of Katrina. If it had, no wonder the woman had gone back to her need to dice Simone into pieces. She shivered.

She climbed onto the big empty bed and paused thinking of Fallyn. She imagined she could still smell his enticing male scent in her nostrils as if she was a shifter like him. While trying to wipe him out of her head enough to allow her to sleep, she heard the front door open. Someone strolled purposely across the floor seeming to be headed toward her bedroom.

Simone grinned and leaped to the floor. Artan would take her mind off his brother. After flying to the door, she wrenched it open and fell into strong arms. He was already hard as a rock, and he engulfed her in an embrace so tight, her breath whooshed from her lungs.

"What is wrong?" he whispered in that familiar tone. But then she frowned. The voice was too cool, too form— She glanced up into the dark eyes of Fallyn and not Artan. She opened her mouth to ask him what he was doing there, but Fallyn swept her up to his hard chest and covered her mouth with a kiss. His greedy hunger was apparent in the way he devoured her, moaning softly, pushing his tongue between her lips.

When he broke off, he didn't give her space but instead, he nuzzled along her neck and gave her small nips that sent chills of pleasure racing over her skin. Simone shuddered in desperate need in his arms. "You shouldn't do this."

"Make me stop, Simone," he murmured at her throat. "Tell me you do not want my touch." He wasn't challenging her, she realized. Fallyn almost begged for her to make him leave, but she couldn't do it. One touch, and she was his.

His hand slipped up her thigh under her nightie, and he squeezed her ass. She sucked in a deep breath. Since she hadn't expected anyone, she hadn't bothered putting panties on. Fallyn's fingers brushed her wet pussy, and she moaned in his arms.

He carried her over to the bed and deposited her there on her back. Her legs were spread, and she knew he could see her naked pussy. His eyes lit on it like it was a special treat created just for him. "Last chance."

Even as he spoke the words, he dropped down on the bed with his face near her center. Simone panted. Was he kidding? She wanted to forget every issue that stood between them and just enjoy his tongue. Fallyn's head swept lower. He breathed her in, eyes closed.

"I know your scent," he murmured. "It is intoxicating. How can this be?" He licked her once, and her cream flowed. He was lost with that taste, evidenced by the way he lapped at her. Simone cried out. She raised her hips up to him, and he gripped her ass as he fed himself. When he sucked on her clit, she scratched at the bed. Fallyn nosed between her slick folds to eat more of her, and Simone gave it up. She raised her legs as high as she could so her heat was exposed. Fallyn didn't lift his head again. He feasted over and over until she came shaking in his hold.

Dimly, through her haze of pleasure, she heard the door open and close. Artan stood at the foot of the bed. Simone was too weak to invite him to join them, but he seemed content to watch. After he'd made her come a second time, Fallyn rose up on his knees and shed his clothes. She stared at his amazing body, wanting to taste him like he'd licked her.

Fallyn crawled up the bed until he reached her head. He threw a muscled thigh up over her and then took hold of his cock. She gasped when he put a hand behind her head and lifted it. "Suck my cock, Simone."

She did as she was told, stretching her mouth wide to accommodate his thick, long shaft. Fallyn groaned as he watched her suck. He leaned down and massaged her breasts, alternating between pinching the nipples.

"Harder," he demanded.

She worked him more, slurping and sucking his full length. She licked his balls and took them into her mouth one at a time and then returned to his cock. He whispered encouragement, firm and commanding. He let her bring him to the edge of an orgasm before he pulled out of her mouth.

For an instant, he flicked his gaze to his brother, but then focused back on Simone. Fallyn moved down the bed and raised one of her legs. He lifted it high enough so he could reach her ass, and he spanked it with one swift, sharp smack. She yelped, and he caressed the area. His fingers slipped up to her pussy, and he pushed two deep into her snatch. Simone writhed under his touch. When she opened her eyes, which had fluttered closed, she found Artan had shifted closer. Now he too was naked. She looked from one to the other. The anticipation to have them inside of her was overwhelming, but they made no move to take her.

"Get up, and take that off," Fallyn instructed. "I want to see you naked."

She rolled to her knees and lifted her nightie over her head. Before she cleared it of her arms, she heard Artan's sharp intake of breath. Her breasts had bounced free of the garment, her nipples puckered into tight buds. His gaze locked on them, and he licked his lips. Simone grinned at him, tilting her head in invitation. But Fallyn was still in charge.

"Go and suck my brother's cock. Get him ready to enter you. I want you on your knees, and I want to see your pussy wet for me while you do it."

She crawled to the end of the bed on her hands and knees. Her back was arched, which raised her ass. Legs slightly apart, she looked over her shoulder at Fallyn. Yeah, he could see all right. The man's gaze never left her body. She turned and took Artan into her mouth. His shaft needed no prep at all. He was already erect. She sucked him anyway, loving the way he tasted in her mouth and the way he made her have to open wider to fit him in. She moaned, and she sucked and licked his cock head. Artan cupped her head, drawing her closer. His breath hissed between his teeth.

She was really getting into licking him from base to tip until she felt Fallyn behind her eating her out. He squeezed her thighs and drew her into his mouth. He ran his tongue from the base of her pussy all the way down to her clit. But instead of taking it into his mouth, he blew on it. He nuzzled the swollen bud with his lips. The movements made her ache to be consumed, but he only teased her.

She paused in sucking Artan and held him in her fist. "Please, Fallyn, suck it," she pleaded.

He ignored her pleas. In fact, he smacked her ass once. She whined. He smacked her stinging cheek again. Her pussy clenched, and she bit her lip. Without warning, Fallyn flipped around so that he was on the edge of the bed with Simone on his lap. Artan dropped back a step, and Fallyn raised her up a little. He brought her down on his erection and impaled her. Not pausing a beat, he began grinding deep into her channel with an arm slung around her middle. Simone hung from his hold, unable to control anything. She could enjoy the sensations and gasp at his roughness, but nothing more.

"Suck him," he demanded.

Half dazed with lust, Simone reached for Artan again, and this time she kept sucking his cock while Fallyn ravaged her pussy. Her umpteenth orgasm built to a frenzy. She moaned around Artan's cock head, and when he exploded into her mouth, she drank him while careening into her own climax.

Fallyn thumped his brother to move, and he did. He popped her off his lap and stood. She was shuffled over to the wall, and he raised her arms as she faced it, legs wide. "Arch," he told her. She did. "More." She rose up on her tiptoes and pushed her ass out as far as she could get it.

Fallyn stepped back, and Artan came up. He kissed along her neck and captured her lips while he worked his cock in one hand. She moaned when he ran the other over her belly and then up to her breasts. All the time, they didn't stop tongue kissing, but it didn't take long for him to be hard enough to take her. He released her mouth and moved behind her. Simone cried out as Artan gripped her hips and shoved his big cock into her pussy. He bent his knees so he could get himself deeper and then he began a slow rhythm that turned into pounding. She screamed his name, no longer caring who might be listening.

After a few minutes, Fallyn tapped his shoulder. Artan pulled out, and his brother replaced him to pump deep inside her. They alternated over and over, wearing her little snatch out, but she didn't care. She came repeatedly as they touched her sweet spot or played with her clit. When she could no longer hold herself up, they did it for her. Simone lost track of time and the number of orgasms. Late into the night, she sagged in Fallyn's arms as he carried her to the bubble bath that Artan had prepared. He climbed in with her and settled beneath the warm surface. Artan took the other end, and together they washed her.

"What am I going to do?" she asked Fallyn sleepily.

He didn't answer, but the twins did exchange a look she couldn't interpret. Much later, she lay between her two bears and fell into a deep slumber.

CHAPTER TEN

Simone woke the next day with neither man in her bed. She'd expected as much from Fallyn but not Artan. Every muscle in her body ached as she sat up, and she stretched. A small noise caught her attention. Simone glanced around the room and discovered she wasn't alone. Tucking the sheet under her arms to cover her nakedness, she glared at Katrina.

"How did you get in here?"

Katrina waved her hand. "We're a close-knit clan. No one uses locks. We don't need them as the crime rate is zero."

Simone had noticed when Katrina first showed up in Charlotte she had a lot more understanding of how things worked in the outside world than Artan and Fallyn did. They might spend most of their time out in the wild, but she bet any amount of money, Katrina didn't.

"You haven't answered my question. I know you don't live here, so what do you want?" She remembered how the woman was ready to end her existence a couple days ago, so she wrapped the sheet around herself and stood up. Scanning the room, she looked for something to defend herself if Katrina decided to forget Fallyn's command to leave her alone. The lamp by the bed looked sturdy enough.

"Relax. I'm not going to attack you." The satisfaction of getting Simone riled was clear in Katrina's expression. "I came to tell you to stay away from Fallyn."

Simone waited for something more, like a threat or an insult, but that seemed to be all the woman had. "Are you serious? That's it? Look I know you want him. You might even love him, but it's obvious to me he doesn't feel the same."

Katrina surged to her feet. "You don't know anything about me—or him! That's what you whores tell yourselves to feel better about stealing someone else's man."

Simone blinked at her a second. "Oh no you did not just call me a whore, bitch!" She forgot about Katrina being a shifter and cracked a palm across her face. Katrina stumbled back and banged against the wall. She growled and came at Simone but stopped inches away with her fingers curved for attack. Her eyes blazed with her anger, and if her abilities extended to visual rays, Simone would be dead where she stood. After some deep breaths, she dropped her arms to her sides and took a few steps back.

"I'm not going to sink to your level," she quipped.

Simone fought not to smack her again. If she did, Katrina might forget Fallyn's warning. She was only willing to push the woman so far.

"You don't care about him," Katrina insisted. "I do. We grew up together. It was expected that—"

"Expected," Simone interrupted. "Y'all keep saying that, but Artan also told me about the mate thing, how it's destined." She sighed, trying to calm down. "Look, I see that you care about him, and I'm sorry if you were hurt with him coming after me."

"Yeah, right." Katrina looked out the window.

"Before I came to Charlotte, my cousin Ayana would talk to me about her man, her baby, as she called him. She said he was so perfect. What surprised her wasn't her feelings for him because he was so hot and so amazing, she couldn't help falling in love. What confused her was how devoted he was to her, like she'd actually been born for him and was so right in every way that he couldn't imagine his life without her. No, not just couldn't—*wouldn't*. At the time, I thought she was talking about one man, and I think she said it like that on purpose 'cause she wasn't ready to let the family know she had two permanent lovers. But since I've been here, I've seen it for myself. Blaine and Reece treat her like she's a gift to them, and they call her their mate. That to me shows how deep this mating thing goes. And you want to ignore all that because 'it's expected.'"

If Simone thought her long speech would impact Katrina's stubbornness, she was so wrong. Her face had grown redder as Simone spoke, and her lips, so thin already, grew thinner. "In other words, you want what your cousin has. Two men."

"Oh come on," Simone growled.

Katrina moved up on her. "You don't care about Fallyn, and you sure don't care about our ways. They're out there hunting right now like all the men and some of the women do almost every day, and what are you doing? Lying here like some princess waiting to be served."

Simone burst out laughing. "Princess. Are you for real? Girl, please, you don't know me any better than I know you. I come from the ghetto where we didn't have anything and sometimes didn't know where our next meal was coming from. And you talk to me about being a princess? I had to work from the day I was old enough to do it. Odd jobs, whatever I could get. You must be crazy. Don't talk to me about what I'm doing. Okay, so I can't hunt or whatever they're doing, but neither can Tammy."

Katrina flared her nostrils in disgust. Simone had to give her that one. Nobody that she'd seen was fooled by that woman.

"I want him to be happy," she finally conceded. "If he'll be that here with you, fine. I…I'm willing to leave with Artan, and then I won't be a temptation to Fallyn. I think Artan can be happy with me wherever we are."

Her words took them both by surprise. Katrina stared at her as if she judged whether Simone was serious. Simone couldn't believe she was talking like it was a done deal her being with Artan from now on. They hadn't been together that long, but she had to admit, she wasn't willing to let him go. And hell, if it didn't work out, he could always come back here, and he could visit with his family any time. She wouldn't hold him back.

Katrina walked over to the door saying nothing. She put her hand on the knob and stopped with her back to Simone. When she turned around, she snarled at Simone making her jump. "I don't believe you for a second, but we'll see what happens. You're right. I do care about him. I love him. If you leave, he'll stop sniffing around you, and we can build a life together. You better keep your word."

Simone ignored the threat and went to the suitcase she had brought with her and not yet unpacked. With effort, she kept her back to Katrina in a clear message of dismissal. The woman's glare burned into Simone. And then as quietly as she had apparently entered the house, she left.

When she had dressed, Simone searched the kitchen for something to eat. She'd been surprised that Artan and Fallyn even had a place, but she supposed everyone else did even if they spent little time there. What didn't surprise her was the fact that there wasn't a speck of food for her to eat. As Katrina had said, the men had gone hunting. She could just imagine them dragging gross dead animals for the women to clean and cook. "Yeah, no thanks."

As she left the house to stand on the front porch, she had to admit deciding to leave Fallyn here and return to her life was the best choice. She might never fit in here. Not that she thought she'd be like what Katrina had accused her of, being a princess. But she couldn't see herself preferring all this to the city. Last night, even though she was tired, the sounds of the night around her woke her up, and the only way to sleep was to bury her head beneath Artan's big arm and bring her knees up to rest on Fallyn's back. It was crazy, but it had worked.

While she stood on the porch sure there was no 7-Eleven nearby to grab a coffee and a greasy breakfast, she watched a young boy run toward her. His hair was wild to match his wide-spaced hazel eyes, and she had a feeling he allowed his eyes to look that way—halfway between human and bear. From the look of it, he enjoyed being what he was and would have it no other way. Now that she thought of it too, there weren't many kids running around. The area was mostly older adults. Maybe this boy was another miracle baby.

"You have to come to Carl's house for breakfast," he told her when he stopped at the foot of the wooden steps.

Simone put her hand on her hip although she wasn't mad at all. "Who says?"

"Carl. My mom goes in and cooks for him and *her*. She made enough for you too. I'll show you the way if you forgot." He raised an eyebrow. "Or are you scared of me?"

She sucked her teeth. "Boy, please, you're just a cub. If you were any threat, you'd have gone hunting with the men."

He growled, giving a great imitation of a bear, and she smiled.

"I'm going next year. You watch and see," he announced.

Simone stepped off the porch. "Yeah, you probably will. If I were your mother, I wouldn't let you go until you were thirty-five. But don't tell me. It's natural for your kind to be out there at like what…eight?"

"Nine!"

"'Scuse me." She laughed. "So you don't like 'her' huh?"

He rolled his eyes giving a good impression this time of Simone. "No, she's human."

"So am I." He said nothing as if his point was made. Simone considered smacking the back of his head, but didn't know how protective his mother was. She wanted to ask him more questions, but the walk to Carl's house was a short one. The little boy left her at the door and scrambled off in another direction. Apparently, he wasn't eating with them.

When she knocked, someone called out "come in" from the other side, and she opened the door. The scent of bacon, sausage, and syrup assaulted her nose. She hoped eggs would also be on the menu. After last night's romp with the twins, she was starving.

"Simone, my dear," Carl bellowed when she entered the dining room. He was already at the head of the table, and he rose, opening his arms.

"Good morning," she murmured and took a seat, ignoring the signal for a hug. Artan wasn't here to drag him off of her, and she wasn't falling for that again. The man could grope his damn wife.

"Hm, not a morning person, huh?" he observed. "Coffee."

The bellow was aimed toward the door she knew led to the kitchen, and it opened to the same woman from last night. Simone looked into her face and saw the little boy's features. So this was his mother.

"Tammy not joining us?" Simone asked.

"She's never up before noon or one," he told her.

"And you don't go on the hunt?"

He frowned. "Not as much since I'm getting up in age. It's all fun for the younger ones anyway. They have a lot more energy. You'll see when they come back and everyone gets together at the lake." Simone resisted putting up a hand to cover her breasts when she noticed his gaze locked on them. "Did you bring a bathing suit?"

"No, I didn't know we would be here that long or that there would be a lake nearby." *And I'm not giving you the satisfaction!*

The grin on his face widened to lecherous quality. Simone tried not to vomit in her mouth.

"No problem. You can always go in the buff."

"In your perverted dreams," she said with as much bluntness as she could. He blinked in surprise at her rudeness.

"W-What?"

"You heard me."

His face reddened. He'd picked up his knife and fork to tuck into the food on his plate, but now he laid them down. She thought he would yell at her or tell her she was ungrateful and rude for a guest. If she landed hungry on her ass at the front porch, she wouldn't have been surprised. The annoyance he felt from her calling him on his disgusting ways was plain. But as soon as he opened his mouth, heels clicked on the hardwood floor just outside of the room.

Carl's lips snapped together, and they both looked around to see Tammy come strolling into the room with high-heeled slip-on shoes with that fluffy stuff on the front. She wore a filmy nightgown that came down to just above her knees, and over that she had a wrap hanging open that was almost as thin as the gown. Simone had to be grateful for the thicker material over her breasts, not so much on the outline of her nipples.

She spun away and swallowed. These people were over-the-top. No wonder the twins stayed in frickin' caves. She might be driven to one inside a week if she had to stay out here. Simone sighed in relief when Ayana followed Tammy into the room. Her cousin took the seat beside her, and Simone squeezed her hand under the table.

"Darling, what are you doing up so early?" Carl asked Tammy. His tone was a demand, but he tried to make it sweet with a tight smile.

Tammy glared at him as she took the seat across the table from Simone. "Two young women in the house?" She shook her head. "I know you, Carl. I had to wake up early to protect them." *Or protect your investment*, Simone mused.

The rest of the meal went fine with Simone chatting with Ayana and Artan and Fallyn's parents, but she missed the twins. When the conversation didn't directly include her, she took the time to consider what she'd said to Katrina. She was serious, and the more she considered it, the firmer she got. She wasn't right for Fallyn, and there was nothing wrong with him thinking about what was important for his people's future. She intended to give him up. She would tell Artan he could come to Charlotte if he wanted to, and then she'd ask Blaine to take her home. There was no sense staying out here any longer than necessary. That would make it harder on all three of them.

She planned to go down to the lake with everyone else and enjoy one last day with both Artan and Fallyn. Then it would be all over. With that thought, she choked on her food, and maybe a sob.

Ayana pounded her back. “You okay?”

Simone’s eyes watered, but she hoped her cousin would blame it on food going down the wrong pipe. “Fine, thanks.” She tilted her head away from Ayana’s probing stare and finished her meal. When she was done, she stood. “Thanks for the food. It was delicious. I’m going to go wait for Artan and Fallyn at their place.”

She left before anyone could question her watery, lopsided smile.

CHAPTER ELEVEN

Simone stuck a toe in the chilly water. She stood on a raft made of tree logs tied together with thick rope. Artan had carried her out on his shoulders. A lightweight pair of shorts and a T-shirt made up her outfit. Earlier, she'd been happy to see a few of the others in his clan wore the same type of clothes. A couple of the women wore bathing suits, and of course Tammy being who she was wore a thong. Several of the men's eyes were glued to her butt, but not Ayana's men or the twins.

Out of nowhere, Artan broke the surface of the water and grabbed her leg. She shrieked and kicked water in his face. "You loser. You scared me."

He chuckled. "That's better. You've been down ever since we got back." He hoisted himself up by flat palms, and she enjoyed another glimpse of how strong he was. She'd never get tired of that. "What's wrong?"

She shrugged. "Nothing."

"Simone," he warned.

"Fine. I'm thinking about leaving."

"No!"

She jumped at the anger mingled with anguish in his tone. He sounded like Fallyn, but she looked out over the water and saw him doing laps with the cook's little boy. She missed him even though he was right there and wished he would come over. His gaze had been on her most of the day since they all came down here, but he didn't stay in her vicinity long. To her surprise, Katrina kept her distance. Simone realized she was giving Simone the time to break it off. The problem was doing it hurt like hell. Why did she have to let go? Why couldn't she have gone for the kind of man who loved the city like she did? At least it wasn't New York, for cripes sake.

Artan ran his hand along her thigh and slipped it between them. She had the feeling he was trying to distract her from her thoughts. "I love your skin," he said when she shivered. "It's so dark and rich, so brown. I love the taste of it on my tongue."

She leaned into him. "Yours isn't so bad either," she teased. The back of her hand rested on his bare chest. He wore shorts and nothing else, and Tammy had mentioned to her that if she and Ayana weren't there, many of them would swim in the nude. She didn't think she'd want some other woman's eyes on Artan and Fallyn's naked bodies, especially Katrina's.

"So, if I stood up right here and took off all my clothes, would you have a problem with it?" she asked him.

The insatiable man's lust lit his eyes, and he looked at her like he could already see her naked. "I wouldn't mind."

Simone frowned. "You don't care if other men see me naked?"

"Not here, no. Everyone respects the fact that you are my mate." For a second his gaze darted in the direction of his father, sunning under a tree having not set one foot in the direction of the water. "I don't care if a man looks as long as he doesn't touch. However, in Charlotte, no. It wouldn't happen."

"Oh it *wouldn't* happen, huh?" She laughed.

"No, it wouldn't." He was just as calm as he pleased about that. Artan might be sweet most of the time, but she saw little glimpses of his dominance, and she didn't mind.

"Well I'll take it a step further," she told him. "I don't want you to be naked at all in front of another woman—here or in Charlotte." And then she fell silent, looking out over the water.

Artan turned her head to force her to look at him. "Tell me you're not leaving us, Simone."

She lowered her eyes. "I-I…"

Without a word he stood up and whipped her onto his shoulders. He waded through the water. At the deeper part, he swam with powerful strokes. Simone couldn't believe he could handle her sitting as she was without him drowning, but soon they were at the shore. Artan didn't put her down but instead carried her into the trees. Soon the shouts of his clan members were left behind, and he set down on a bent tree bark with her propped on his lap.

"Talk to me," he commanded.

Simone twisted her hands together. Not because she was scared to talk to him, but because she never wanted to hurt either him or his brother. Doing that felt like more than she could bear, and it brought her to the realization that she loved him and Fallyn. She didn't want to let Fallyn go but she would, if it was best for him.

To her shame and embarrassment, she started to cry, and Artan whipped her around to engulf her in his strong arms. She laid her head on his shoulder, sniffing and trying to pull herself together.

"I love you," she whispered, digging her nails into his arms. He gently removed them and folded her hands on her lap. "Oh, sorry."

He tipped her chin up. "I love you too, and it shouldn't make you cry to know that."

"I know, but…" She licked her lips. "Artan, I'm going to leave here. I don't like it out here. I'm so sorry. I'm selfish and horrible, and it makes me ashamed to feel like this. You deserve better, but I'm not going to pretend either. I like the city. Or I guess I should say I like the suburbs where Ayana lives. I'm going to try to get something in that area. Maybe not a house because I can't afford that much yet. But—"

He cut off her words and kissed her lips. Simone gave into him, molding her body to his and wrapping her arms around his neck. This time, she wasn't so tense that she tried to carve him like a turkey with her fingernails.

When he drew back, he looked into her eyes. His expression was so gentle, she wanted to cry again. None of her previous boyfriends or any men she'd met back home had been as sweet and caring as Artan.

"Wherever you go, Simone, I will go. Do you understand?"

"I can't be that selfish. I—"

He put a finger over her lips. "Wherever you go, I go. End of story. I can visit my family whenever I like, but I will be with you. Besides, I like learning about Charlotte, and Blaine and Reece will keep me company. So what else?"

She hesitated, and she saw him look past her for a second before focusing on her again. She'd known Artan would feel this way, but it had still made her nervous thinking about it until he actually said it. Fallyn was a whole other story.

"Fallyn," she began.

"What about him?" he coaxed. When she didn't say anything, he said, "You don't love him?"

She closed her eyes. Her voice was so low, it was a wonder Artan didn't lean in to hear her even though she was right there on his lap. "I love him so much, I feel like I can't breathe when I think about leaving him."

Remembering that Katrina was the one who was right for Fallyn hurt worse and didn't strengthen her resolve in the least. But she'd made her decision, so it didn't matter. Besides, Fallyn had chosen. He said from the beginning he wouldn't make her his mate.

Simone closed her eyes and stiffened her spine. "Katrina is the one for him, so I'm not going to let him touch me anymore. Because I've been so weak, I think it's better if I leave right away. And when you come up here to visit, I'm not coming with you. I hope you can accept that, Artan, because it's all I've got."

"No."

She looked up at him, but Artan hadn't been the one to speak. She twisted around on his lap and found Fallyn behind them. She knew right away that he'd heard their entire conversation. Artan had been looking at his brother when he glanced away from her. She sighed.

"Don't start, Fallyn. I'm giving you what you want, and if you think I'm not right for Artan, then you can take it up with him."

He walked over and pulled her from Artan's arms. His twin let her go and stood. Simone fought to get his hands off of her, but she was a trapped animal beneath his strong hands. His black eyes seemed to burn on her flesh, and she shook in his hold. *Come on, Simone, you're made of harder stuff than this, damn it. Pull your ass together.* But she couldn't. She cried some more.

"You are not leaving me," Fallyn ground out.

Simone's mouth fell open. "Come again?"

To her shock, his forehead touched hers, and he closed his eyes. "You are my mate. I love you, and I am not letting you go, Simone."

"I…I…But I don't understand. You said—"

"I was a fool who needed change but did not want to embrace it. I thought I was stronger than my ancestors who could never have denied their mate. I am not. You are meant for me, and I will spend my life with you—wherever that may be."

Simone reached up and cupped both sides of his face with her hands. She rose up on tiptoes to kiss him and nuzzle close to him. Her heart pounded, and blood rushed in her ears. She could hear nothing beyond their panting breaths as they devoured one another. With every taste of his lips, she wondered how she could have walked away. His arms around her seemed to give her life, and she didn't think she could bear it to be away from him.

She gave him one last out. "I don't want you to be unhappy."

"I will not be." He gripped her tighter to his chest.

"What about Katrina? Will she accept it if you choose me?" Something told her that Katrina wasn't going for anything Simone had to say. She'd made that nice little speech back at their house about how she was going to leave Fallyn and go back to Charlotte. He'd blown that little plan to bits, and Simone couldn't help the joy that sprung up inside of her. "I'm not like her, Fallyn. I mean I can deal with anything when I'm with you and Artan. But maybe she's more right for you."

"Whether she is or she is not does not matter. I have chosen you, and there is no other woman that I want. I will follow you wherever you go." Simone thought she heard a feminine cry somewhere nearby, but her whole attention was for the man in front of her. Then Artan moved in close to his brother's side, and the devotion she saw in their eyes overwhelmed her.

She put a trembling hand in each other theirs, and one man kissed along the left side of her throat, and the other caressed the right side with his lips. She sagged into their arms, and they raised their heads to look at her again. In that instant, she knew nothing else was as important as Artan and Fallyn. Clothes and hair and manicures or pedicures didn't amount to anything. Not family or friends, not the city or the country. No one but the two of them.

"I think it doesn't matter where I am, whether I'm here or back home. As long as you two are with me, I'm okay. I will follow you wherever you go." A tear slipped down her cheek, and Fallyn reached up to wipe it away.

His amused grin broke the mushy intensity of the moment. "We will go to Charlotte."

Artan chuckled and tugged Simone into his arms. "Yes, tomorrow."

Simone let out a relieved *whoop* and ran off in the direction of the house with twin sexy bear shifters in hot pursuit.

The End

About the Author

Tressie Lockwood has always loved books, and she enjoys writing about heroines who are overcoming the trials of life. She writes straight from her heart, reaching out to those who find it hard to be completely themselves no matter what anyone else thinks. She hopes her readers enjoy her short stories. Visit Tressie on the web at www.tressielockwood.blogspot.com.

11995460R00134

Made in the USA
Lexington, KY
16 November 2011